NEVERTHELESS

Renelle Marie

authorHOUSE®

AuthorHouse™
1663 Liberty Drive
Bloomington, IN 47403
www.authorhouse.com
Phone: 1-800-839-8640

First published by AuthorHouse   4/21/2011

ISBN: 978-1-4567-3486-2 (sc)
ISBN: 978-1-4567-3487-9 (hc)
ISBN: 978-1-4567-3488-6 (e)

Library of Congress Control Number: 2011901886

Printed in the United States of America

Any people depicted in stock imagery provided by Thinkstock are models, and such images are being used for illustrative purposes only. Certain stock imagery © Thinkstock.

This book is printed on acid-free paper.

CHAPTER ONE

Dusk was always her favorite time of day—that calming transition from the day's rapid work pace toward evening's darkness that eased into night's rest. Savoring dusk outside in pleasant weather isn't always possible in this busy world, but whenever achievable for her, Ilana couldn't help but to cherish it. She was soon to realize, however, that a better-thought-out plan would never have her alone in a strange uninhabited place during her favorite time of day.

"All patients are stable in here now!" someone had called from between swinging doors, and a unanimous sigh could be heard emanating from everyone in the ICU waiting room. Ilana's volunteer duties involved giving patient updates to worried families, so she always shared their relief when they heard the word. Ilana was free to leave whenever the declaration was made close to the end of her commitment time, but today's earlier-than-usual exit gave her an unexpected opportunity. She could take advantage of the remaining daylight in this near winter time in the South to investigate what kept sneaking into and capturing her thoughts the entire day.

"Ms. Hayes, you've been so helpful today, and I just wanted you to know how much we appreciate your kindness," an older woman graciously told Ilana.

"Oh, you're so welcome; glad to help. I'll be here again in the morning to do whatever I can." After saying her goodbyes and gathering her things, Ilana signed out and quickly left to find her small car in the hospital parking garage.

She anxiously headed to where she'd seen something unusual that morning, on obviously long-neglected property—a bright yellow spot she'd never noticed before. It had apparently been completely hidden until a now-toppled tree exposed it. It might be nothing of any consequence and she couldn't even explain her interest, but curiosity compelled her to investigate, though she was hardly dressed for a trek in the woods.

The wind of the previous night's rainstorm dramatically changed the landscape she loved. Trying to spot damage during that morning's commute, while keeping a watchful eye on this curved levee-lined road, had been challenging. Seeing hanging limbs on leaning trees had depressed her then, and this evening's reverse ride oppressed her all over again in its replay. *Nevertheless*, the rain had completed its necessary cleansing, leaving the air fresh-smelling and the grass and leaves glistening.

Because she loved seeing the tree-filled properties road-side, Ilana always preferred driving on this La.18—River Road, instead of the main highway. She'd become very familiar with this special road that ran parallel to the Mississippi River on its west side, for she'd driven it several times a week since her divorce. On the river side was a grass-covered levee that runners, bicyclers, and dogs and their walkers enjoyed.

On the other side was what had always fascinated Ilana—the land that was now newly wind-damaged. She envisioned the possible history of those varied properties, along with that of their owners. Some were spacious areas graced by stately plantation homes and some held more meager houses. Trailers were on some, usually to be replaced by large beautiful homes, probably when the owners had adequate funds to build them. There were also lonely barren areas where older homes once stood, sad now because all that was visible were columns on either side of where a driveway entrance had obviously been. In the center of some of the properties stood fireplaces and hearths that refused to succumb to the probable fires that apparently overtook the houses. Speckling the landscape along the way were varying sizes of all types of trees, the older ones draped in Spanish moss that the river breezes lifted gracefully—always a wondrous sight.

When Ilana approached the area that piqued her unrestrained curiosity, she slowed and cautiously turned off onto the next road past the property. She chose a parking spot she hoped solid enough to prevent her from getting stuck in the rain-caused muck. For a fleeting moment she thought someone might find a strange little blue car there somewhat odd and worried her trespassing might get her into trouble. However, she quickly dismissed her concerns when she reconsidered, sad as it is, people don't take time to notice things that don't directly affect them.

After retrieving her flashlight from the glove compartment, she locked the car and headed toward where she recalled seeing it—a tiny bright yellow spot. Her anxious steps crushed underbrush that crackled and disturbed surrounding life, causing scampering sounds she hoped were squirrels or rabbits. Adrenaline urged her forward. She wouldn't allow herself fear that snakes might be what she heard, since she held only a flashlight weapon in her hand and a strong determination in her heart.

As she maneuvered over a huge wet toppled tree trunk, she was thankful she'd chosen to wear pants and low-heeled shoes that morning instead of a skirt and heels. When each twig-breaking step eventually put her deep into the property, she could periodically catch glimpses of yellow, though vague behind dark brush. It became her tiny beacon to follow while climbing over more branches. After pushing aside high brush and coming to a clearing, the yellow was close enough for her to recognize it as a mere piece of bright cloth at roof height. It might be a blown-loose piece of trash or the remains of a child's unsuccessful kite flight. Suddenly something else it could also be sprung to mind...something less innocent. Oh not that! She didn't even want to think of it! Could it possibly be the remnants of crime-scene tape?

Dwelling on that last revelation caused immediate thoughts of 'what in the world am I doing here?' She felt her heartbeats accelerate, for it was apparent darkness would soon be upon her and her flashlight then her only visible light. She struggled to advance more swiftly, determined not to be deterred by this added intrigue—not after coming this far. She finally got near enough to see that the yellow fabric was attached to the top corner of a long side wall on an obviously unused structure. Most of the visible front wall, weathered gray by time, was leaning inward under vines. She approached the structure's farthest corner to find the back wall completely upright and attached to what seemed like a porch that spanned the wall's entire length.

Suddenly, she made the abrupt decision to turn around, quickly retrace her steps, and head back to the car, for an abnormally large angry hissing cat sat alert at the porch corner. An adamant dog lover, Ilana seriously distrusted cats! Positive she preferred unknown scampering sounds to that awful loud hissing, she backtracked her way to the car. The same huge tree trunk confirmed she was headed in the right direction, and soon after stumbling over it, she spotted her shiny blue home on wheels—a comforting sight!

Ilana's drive home was entirely automatic, for she could think of nothing but where she'd just been. This was her usual day of the week to stop at the carwash, her only real luxury since the divorce. She normally did a crossword puzzle while waiting for the car to be washed and vacuumed, something previously done by her ex in the driveway every weekend. The carwash was one of many things she passed right by, for today she was oblivious to everything but an overwhelming feeling of accomplishment.

Once safely in her townhouse and able to entertain other thoughts, Ilana became intensely aware of uncomfortable stinging on her feet and arms from scratches she didn't realize she had. Looking down, she also discovered that her impetuous adventure had probably destroyed her favorite shoes. So exhilarated by having been on a River Road property, however, she wouldn't allow scratches and ruined shoes to concern her.

While dabbing cotton swabs of peroxide on her scratches, she reflected on her favorite areas along her usual commute, those similar to where she'd just been, those untouched by humanity for many years. What she especially loved about those unkempt tracts of land were the massive evergreen oak trees. Even in the coldest weather, they seemed to explode above blankets of gray brush like billowing mushroom-shaped emeralds. Maybe they sprouted by chance long ago, but Ilana knew some were planted—possibly by a husband and wife.

The couple might have deliberated a long time before deciding on the perfect locations for the trees. Maybe years later, the couple's children happily enjoyed a tree swing their father hung from a majestic tree branch. Whether intentionally planted or assisted by a squirrel or bird, to Ilana those oaks were true examples of inspiration, simply for having survived years of abuse from winds and possible floods. They might have even inspired her to risk searching the property today and now wanting to further investigate its entire perimeter—despite that awful hissing cat.

Realizing suddenly how famished she was, Ilana quickly gathered ingredients and began whipping some eggs for a cheese and green onion omelet. She intended to re-treat her scratches as it cooked but was disturbed by a phone call.

"Ms. Hayes," the voice said, "I've been told the lovely music I recently heard at a friend's funeral was your CD. It so helped my friend get through her husband's services that I'd like to buy it for her in hopes it may comfort her further."

"Yes, I can see that you get one. The CDs are organ/harp duets my friend and I recorded, and people do seem to prefer them to live music in order to keep them as a memory. If you'll give me your address and credit card number, I'll send you one."

"Actually I'd like to buy whatever other CDs you have since I've heard the wedding one also. Everyone at the weddings I've attended thought the music made the weddings even nicer."

"Thank you, but there are only two—one for weddings and one for funerals."

"Oh, I was so hoping you'd recorded more. I guess I'll have to settle for one of each, the wedding one for my engaged niece. I've got interested friends who'll also be calling, for we've really enjoyed them both."

"I appreciate that. You should get them soon."

Since word of the CDs had spread throughout the South, Ilana rarely played for weddings and funerals anymore. Actually CD sales, wise post-divorce investing of her share of their home sale, plus her retirement, gave Ilana a sufficient income. Since she knew the dire need for volunteerism, she enjoyed the freedom of filling her four-day weeks with seven-hour days of volunteer work.

After completing the transaction, Ilana sensed how very tired she was. Normally she was spent at the day's end and relaxed watching TV or reading, but today she longed for a relaxing tub soak. After having her omelet and cleaning the kitchen, she proceeded directly toward the bathroom to absorb a soak's soothing comfort—hoping her scratches could handle it.

CHAPTER TWO

Ilana's volunteer work week included Mondays and Tuesdays in the hospital waiting room or the gift shop, and Wednesdays and Thursdays at the animal shelter. She decided to make her second yellow speck pursuit on Friday of the same week, her volunteer-free day, which would allow her an entire day of the sun's complete accompaniment. She awoke that morning thinking she'd make a wiser choice than her previous spontaneous trek had found her wearing. Today she'd be in something suitable for rugged terrain. She might not be able to avoid bruises, but jeans, boots, and a long-sleeved shirt should prevent scratches. After having breakfast and coffee, she figured all areas were covered as she left the townhouse with a stash of sunscreen, mosquito repellant, wasp spray, a flashlight, water, a power health bar, and some gloves.

She turned from the River Road onto the same side road as before, but parked farther back this time. As she trampled toward the back of the structure, squirrels scampered away, alarmed birds chirped and took flight, what sounded like a pounding hammer became more prominent, and a dog barked somewhere nearby.

Before long she came upon a wall opposite the one she'd seen previously. It was attached to what might have been a back porch. Noticing the sound of the hammering seemed closer now than before, Ilana climbed up onto the corner of the porch, fearing it might collapse at any moment. After walking the length of it safely, she could see well enough over bushes to distinguish a small house from which the pounding seemed to come. She was seriously dreading the sight of that same dreadful cat when a tan-colored dog suddenly appeared. It began barking ferociously at something oddly familiar that scampered from under the porch in a furry haze that emitted an angry meowing sound. Immediately Ilana knew she loved this dog!

However, the dog then turned and began barking its way toward her, but she knew it's natural instincts commanded that it guard its turf. As she spoke softly to it, the dog quieted and inched slowly closer, until it seemed to accept her being there. Assuming it belonged to the owners of the house, she expected the dog to return there after being satisfied with her presence. Surprisingly, her new best friend seemed content with joining her as she continued to look around and accompanied her closely.

Ilana soon noticed the hammering had stopped, and, except for some croaking frogs, all was quiet. Suddenly interrupting the silence and startling her came a man's voice in the distance.

"What's goin' on? What're you doin' here?"

She turned to see an older man dressed in khakis and a khaki baseball cap approaching from the direction of the house. Momentarily afraid, *nevertheless,* somehow relieved at seeing another human, she answered, "Oh, sir, I'm so sorry for trespassing. I really have no business being here. I'm only curious and mean no harm."

As the man climbed over brush and came closer, Ilana noticed kind greenish eyes behind scratched glasses, as he said, 'Your bein' here's okay I guess. I live out back. I'm Godfrey Gaudin. But, if you're walkin' on my property, I should know who you are."

"I'm Ilana Hayes and I live here in Riverside. My curiosity got the best of me I guess. On my way to work the other day I saw a speck of yellow from the road, and it was on something I didn't know was there."

"Well, that somethin' was probably what used to be a pretty nice house at one time, but the yellow, I can't say I know what that is."

"It's attached to the other side's corner, on the roof edge. It looks like a piece of fabric and it's pretty bright. I pass here often but never noticed it until after the storm the other night. The wind must have moved things from in front of it."

He seemed to think intently and said, "Let's see, yellow—somethin' yellow. Hmm…Oh, you know, I think I know what it might be. Matter of fact, it's probably somethin' I put there myself. My grandkids loved to run around and play in the old house when it was empty after my parents died. We even put up a Christmas tree in it one year and my little granddaughter had me throw her bright yellow doll blanket up on the roof so Santa would see that house too. I wrapped that little blanket around a rock she found and threw it above the roof as hard as I could. I remember how she jumped and cheered when it stuck. I guess what's left of it made its way over to the corner and got caught. That's a long time ago now."

"Then you lived here with your parents? I've imagined families living along here among all these trees and what it must have been like growing up close to the Mississippi, but I've never really spoken to anyone who lived here."

"Well, imagine that! And here you are, talkin' to one now. Oh we had good times here—my sisters, my brother, my parents, and I—yep, right here in what used to be a house, and it's a levee and a road away from that old Mississippi."

"Do you mind my asking what happened to the house?"

"No, heck, don't mind tellin' you all about it if you want. Let's sit here on this rickety old porch edge." And so they sat and Ilana listened and absorbed all he told her about this house and this sweet Godfrey Gaudin's past. His parents had died many years prior to the time the weather took its toll on the house, actually the fourth one his father built before deciding it was the one just right for his family. Later, Godfrey and his older brother helped him build additions onto it to accommodate his growing family.

"Yep, my dad taught me a lot about construction, and when the girl of my dreams consented to marry me, my dad and I built the house for us in back that I live in now."

Ilana noticed Godfrey's eyes watering as he told her about happy times and reminisced on the sadness of losing his wife. "It's so different since she's gone; a part of me's missing," he said, "even though it's been a while. I've always been kind of a loner, so after she died, I kept to myself and stayed close to home. Oh, I've got two daughters and some grandchildren close by who want me to visit them all the time. They show up here pretty often to check on me, and one of 'em calls every night, but I guess they know I manage pretty well. I raise some vegetables, repair my house as it needs it, watch some TV, and see some old friends down at the diner. You know somethin'? This is the first time I've walked over to this part of the land in a very long time—there's really no need to. Yep, I guess I should probably do somethin' with this property but it's too big a job. I'd first have to clear away the downed trees, and that takes equipment I don't have."

Ilana had listened intently and thoroughly enjoyed all she heard, but wanted to know something else. When he paused, she asked him if they'd ever had a tree swing.

"Oh sure, it was out back on that old oak. You can still see part of the rope hangin'. My own kids used it too. Yep, those were happy times." He wiped his watering eyes with his sleeve, then abruptly rose as he said, "I've been rattlin' on about old memories you young people don't care about when I've got things to do."

Ilana quickly jumped off the porch and said, "I've truly loved hearing it all, really, and would love to hear more if you weren't so busy. You seem like a kind and wise man who truly loves his family."

"I gotta go." Ilana noticed a break in his voice as Godfrey tried to leave. "Come on, you old dog, and get out of the lady's way." Because the dog seemed content to linger, Godfrey had to come closer, close enough for Ilana to see more tears going down his weather-worn face.

Partly to help Godfrey forget his sadness, Ilana asked? "Is that cat yours too? I was really glad your sweet dog scared it off earlier."

Godfrey answered sternly, "This old mutt's not mine and I don't know about a cat. I don't like cats. This old dog just started hangin' around one day after findin' my drippin' hose beside the house, and then wouldn't leave. And he's a she and she ain't so sweet. She went and got herself pregnant. Lil hussy! Animals are nothin' but trouble."

"You know what? That nothin'-but-trouble dog just alerted you by barking to let you know something out of the ordinary was going on over here."

"Yeah, I know, but I don't need protection. I do okay. Hey, if you like that mutt, you could have her. Lord knows I don't give her much attention. I don't even let her inside. I just feed her what I don't eat. She don't even have a name."

"Oh, you must be fond of her a little. I'm such a dog lover that I'd already have a dog if I'd taken some time to think about it. But it's not long that I've been in my new place. Actually, now that I think of it, I've been moved in a while, but I'm still decorating. That's because I'm always decorating. Anyway, my heart does tell me to take her, but I really should think about it. Can I get back to you on it?"

"Sure. I'm here most days. Good talkin' to ya." And he turned to walk away.

"Thank you so much. It's really been a pleasure meeting you. Hey, Godfrey, if I would come back and get her, what do you think about my calling her Blossom?"

"Fine with me—Flower, Grass, Tree, Bush—whatever name you like," he answered while looking down, chuckling, and shaking his head. He then waved and turned back toward his house, the dog following behind him.

CHAPTER THREE

After Godfrey left, Ilana sat on the old porch, slowly sipping her bottled water. Frog and cricket sounds shared the stillness as she thought over all he'd told her. How thankful she was that she'd persisted in investigating that spot of yellow! It resulted in her good fortune of meeting someone with a history here, and, lucky for her, he was someone willing to contribute a narration of it.

She lingered in thought, not able to resist feelings of gratitude for her life now. She was in a wonderful stage, with child-rearing responsibilities over, even though, as all mothers know, concerns always remain. There were so many things she was grateful for, one being her good health, for she'd lost too many friends to cancer. She had the devotion of friends and family, lived in a lovely place, and owned a nice car. *Nevertheless,* she knew what made her life especially nice now was something she'd never known before and was possibly still getting used to—a complete feeling of freedom!

Her two successful children, Amelie and Addison, had finished college and been on their own for a while, a fact that had forced Ilana and their father to face their marital problems with no distractions. Actually they were really only Ilana's marital problems because he was content with their relationship. She was still asounded by the fact that, after all their years together, he didn't know her well enough to notice how unhappy she was. Her friends and children fully understood, however, and supported her in the divorce, once she convinced them she could handle living alone. All agreed she'd be secure in the sturdy, well-insulated townhouse she'd chosen that was close to friends and volunteer work. They also knew she'd manage easily financially because she tended to live simply and didn't require luxuries.

Amelie and Addison had been in Ilana's life daily at the beginning of these post-divorce years, and now they stayed in contact occasionally either by phone or e-mail. Addison Philip, the oldest at 27, lived and worked about two hours away as an architect. He was a tall dark-haired deep thinker whose hobbies were music and cars. Amelie Clare, an adventurous but sensitive nature-lover, was two years younger and worked on animal research about an hour away.

Amelie insisted her mother choose a townhouse that had a connected garage with a remote that would allow her to exit her car once safely inside the townhouse structure. Addison was more interested in—and unusually vocal about it—her assurances that she was being attentive to her car maintenance and keeping her gas tank full.

They were both such a wonderful help to her in the move, for she'd found relocating from their only family home extremely hard. During the packing and the ever-necessary discarding process, Ilana's tears dripped into multiple boxes as she came across reminders of happy family times. Though the move was fairly traumatic, once she was settled comfortably into her new digs, she was immediately content with her aloneness. She was able to decorate to her liking at her leisure, though that stage of relocation seemed to be on-going. Ilana enjoyed finding ways of making the townhouse more pleasant and comfortable for her, her family, and her friends, so she was always improving her surroundings.

During their marriage, Ilana had opted to choose her arguments with her then husband so they'd only have the very necessary ones. As a result, she had long given up the hope of having a dog because of his aversion to it. However, by the time she finally left Godfrey's porch, she had come to the realization that this was the first time in her adult life she could consider dog ownership without having to consult anyone. When she reached her car, she'd firmly decided there was no reason this long-wanted pleasure couldn't become a reality for her—along with the bonus of Blossom offspring.

That decided, Ilana headed to the grocery to pick up some things to fix herself a late, but much nicer lunch, than a power bar. In the townhouse later, while putting away groceries and keeping an eye on her simmering pork chop and vegetables, she couldn't resist the urge to let Amelie and Addison know about Blossom.

Addison, a definite dog lover, was thrilled with the news, not just because he knew it would make his mother happy, but more so because of the protection a dog would provide. He was well aware of how she'd always wanted a house dog, but, as far as he knew, never had one, even in her childhood. He remembered their dad refusing to let Ilana bring home a shelter dog for them, so they grew up with only an occasional stray they'd feed for a while. Because they were never allowed inside, each dog would eventually wander off in search of better protection from the heat and cold.

Amelie, animal-lover extraordinaire, of course wanted to see Blossom as soon as possible and elaborated on all Ilana would need in the townhouse for the new dog family. She also offered Ilana some unexpected insight with, "You know, Mom, mother dogs seem to like familiarity when they deliver. Maybe she shouldn't be moved from her usual surroundings quite yet if she's very far along. It might be best for her to stay at Godfrey's for now so she can be comfortable delivering the pups wherever she's contented sleeping."

After preparing for a dog family the entire weekend, Ilana found Monday's work commitment endless. When 'stable' was finally heard, she went straight to Godfrey's to find Blossom approaching—without a bark. As she knocked on Godfrey's door, she could see through the screen that he was watching TV news. Immediately she was sorry she'd possibly disturbed him, for she realized too late he might have been about to fall asleep. When he turned and saw her, his beaming smile erased any of her previous regrets as he said, "Well, hi lil lady! Come on in and I'll get you some coffee."

"No, Godfrey, that's not necessary. I just wanted to let you know, if it's still okay, I definitely want Blossom. I'd like to take her now and bring her to the vet. I've already called and they're expecting us. There's something I should talk to you about though. When she delivers, she should be in the most comfortable place possible, the place where she'd feel most at ease."

"Oh, really? Uh, sure. What place? You think she cares where she has her pups?"

"Definitely! It's very important that she be in a familiar spot she's well accustomed to, so she won't feel more stress than necessary during delivery."

"What? Oh, okay. We can't have her stressed, I guess."

"Now, where do you usually find her? Where is she most of the time?"

"Well, you know I don't pay her much mind, but I guess right there under that chair on the carport. Yep, that's where she stays. I guess I'd have found her and some pups all under there one mornin' when I came out."

"Would you mind then, if the vet finds her to be far along, that we not disturb her and let her deliver right there? She'd probably be more content there—but with a nice quilt under her, of course."

"It won't bother me none, but I'm sure I don't have a nice enough quilt. You know, Ilana, animals are always havin' their babies with nobody carin' that they're content and at ease. Aren't you bein' just a little finicky about this whole dog-deliverin'-puppies thing?"

"No, I don't think so. I'd like to do whatever can be done to help her."

"Oh, yeah, right! Well, I surely wasn't plannin' to help her. I figure she was gonna handle those mama dog things herself."

"In case there's a problem, I'll get my daughter over here to help when it's time."

Godfrey looked at her very seriously and teased, "Now, let me get this straight! I'm lettin' you have my dog, a dog I took such good care of and I don't even know enough about you to know you have a daughter? You let me go on the other day about me and you didn't tell me anything about your family. Let's have some coffee and you can tell me about 'em, I mean since I'm givin' you my dog."

"Well, if I didn't have to get Blossom to the vet before closing time, I'd surely take you up on that. We could sit out here and I'd bore you pretty good, pictures and all."

"I'd like that a lot," and his broad smile brightened his aged face.

"How about I come back here tomorrow around the same time? I might be bringing Blossom back anyway, depending on what the vet says."

"Wonderful!" he said, and there was that happy smile again.

Ilana had the impulse to hug this sweet old guy, but just touched his shoulder, smiled, and asked, "Are you sure you won't miss Blossom?"

"Whether that dog's here or not don't matter to me. You can have that cat too. I took just as good care of it as I did this old mutt, you know! You sure you don't want that cat too?" and he laughed so good heartedly—like he hadn't in a while.

"No cat! I share your dislike for cats." Ilana called Blossom, got her settled on the passenger side, and drove off saying, "See you tomorrow, with or without Blossom!."

"Don't forget now. I'll have the coffee hot for ya," and he waved his hat, revealing a bald head edged in gray-white fringe atop a happy tanned face.

CHAPTER FOUR

The next morning Godfrey continued his home improvement project he'd abandoned a day ago to investigate dog barking. By late afternoon, one last piece of ceiling molding needed to be installed in the last of the bedrooms he was redoing, and he was determined to put it up before calling it a day. Exhausted, but extremely grateful not to have to climb the ladder again, he descended it for the final time, checked out the finished room, and felt very satisfied with the result. Ravenous by now, yet too tired to cook something, he took a quick shower and walked over to Ed's diner—a short way down River Road—to reward himself with a good meal.

None of his friends he usually had lunch with were around, so he sat alone in a booth, enjoying a big plate of shrimp etouffee, He was happily consuming his favorite dessert, coconut cake, and smiling at how particular Ilana was about the dog, when the voice of someone clearing away his dishes broke into his thoughts, "Man, that cake must really be something special."

"Huh? Oh yeah, it's pretty good but not like my wife used to make," Godfrey responded as he looked up to find a small, long-haired, tanned boy of about nine in torn jeans and a frayed tee shirt that was way too short.

"Oh, she must be gone now huh?" the kid asked, "and you miss her?"

"About ten years now. She was feisty and fussed some, but I miss having her around a lot."

"Man, you let some chick fuss at you?"

"Oh, I fussed back some, but mostly I went along with what she liked all those years. And, by the way, I don't think of her as some chick! How old are you, kid?"

"Oh, uh, I'm sixteen," he answered as he tugged on his tee shirt in a futile effort to lengthen it.

"Come again? You're not even old enough to be workin'."

"Aw, how'd you know? Don't say anything, Mister, please, to make them suspect," the boy pleaded. "I really need the money."

"You do, huh? Well I'd say you better get that hair cut if you want to stay workin'. What's your name, kid?"

"I'm Flex, and I can't afford to get a haircut."

"Flex! Is that short for somethin'? And do you have a last name?"

"Yeah, sure! But what's yours?"

"I'm Godfrey Gaudin. I've never noticed you in here before and I pretty much know everyone in Riverside—but I haven't been in here lately. Where ya live, kid?"

"Well, I've been sleepin' in the kitchen in back since I been workin' here. I just started but I'm here every day. Mister, that cake might not be like your wife's, but it sure does look good."

Recognizing a longing look on the boy's face and ashamed he hadn't noticed it before, Godfrey asked, "Flex, you want some cake? Have you eaten?"

"Well, last night I ate what was left in the kitchen and tonight they'll let me do the same, so I'm okay."

"Yeah, but it's early yet. They won't be closin' for a while. I'll get you a piece of cake. You go tell 'em I'd like another glass of milk and order a big piece of cake and some milk for you, and you sit down here and keep me company while I drink my milk. There aren't any more customers comin' in right now anyway."

"Okay, thanks. I'll ask if it's okay," was the thrilled response as he took away the utensils and cake saucer.

Godfrey began to think how extraordinary things were—spending time with Ilana and now meeting this seemingly lonely, scared kid—oddly amazing in contrast to his normal routine, which was pretty empty and uninteresting. Flex returned shortly, tray in hand and grinning broadly. He set everything down and hungrily ate the cake while gulping down the milk, as Godfrey watched curiously. When Flex slowed down enough, Godfrey questioned him cautiously, while trying not to impose. What he then learned from Flex's account of the past few days made his day thus far seem inconsequential, even boring. Listening in amazement, Godfrey could hardly believe what he heard.

Flex found his way to the diner after bike-riding on the Mississippi River levee for two days. Knowing he'd never be missed at the foster home upriver, he'd left with only an old bike he found on a neighbor's trash pile and some fruit picked from another neighbor's satsuma tree. After pedaling during daylight hours and sleeping when he couldn't pedal any longer, he'd been unable to resist the urge to ride down the levee to the diner when his hunger got the best of him.

Flex told Godfrey how he loved the freedom of being atop the levee and how he had walked it daily this past school term instead of taking the school bus. He explained that he wanted to avoid riding the bus with the other foster kids from the same home because they took advantage of his small size. Maybe because Flex was also the youngest, the foster home kids were further encouraged by the school bus bullies.

For the most part, the kids in the foster home were on their own and looked out for themselves, so no one cared that Flex left early every morning. He confessed it wasn't long before he discovered when he got close enough to the river, he could hear tugboat captains planning their days. Although Flex never saw them, it was apparent to Godfrey by the look on Flex's face, that hearing those voices from the boats every weekday morning was his only enjoyment.

When Godfrey questioned him about his family, he learned that the only person Flex remembered was his grandmother. He thought she must have taught him the few prayers he knew, but mostly he could recall her singing to him. He figured she must have died when he was about five, since he'd been told he was in foster care since then. He knew nothing of his parents.

Godfrey suddenly noticed it had gotten dark out and knew he should be home when his daughter called. He had to interrupt Flex by saying, "Oh, my gosh, one of my kids will be driving over to check on me if they call and I'm not at home. I hate to leave but have to go. I would've liked to stay so we could've talked some more."

As Godfrey rose, Flex thanked him for the cake and milk and asked hopefully, "Will you be back sometime?"

"I come for lunch once in a while, so sure," Godfrey answered as he walked over to the counter to pay Ed, the owner and a long-time friend. Flex was right beside him as Godfrey asked Ed, "Don't you think I should show your new employee where the best barber in Riverside is?"

"That's a great idea, Godfrey!" Ed responded enthusiastically. "He's a good little worker, but could look a little nicer."

Godfrey put his arm around a smiling Flex and said "I'll see you soon."

From what this kid had been through, Godfrey knew sheer necessity to survive had toughened Flex, so he probably wouldn't accept pity. *Nevertheless*, Godfrey intended to find him a place to stay and get him back in school. Ed would be the only other person who might think of helping Flex, but he was always too busy in the diner for extra thoughts—or extra time. Godfrey had much more of that.

During his walk home, Godfrey decided there was no reason Flex couldn't stay with him, since he had two extra bedrooms. The bigger of the two would be perfect, and why wait? He could go over to the diner and talk to him about it the very next day.

When he got his daughter's expected phone call that night, Godfrey asked her to bring over any of his grandson's outgrown clothes she might still have. He also made her promise to bring them before going to work the next morning because he knew he'd have to see Flex in the morning since he expected Ilana in the afternoon. Naturally his daughter was completely bewildered by his request, so Godfrey assured her he'd explain everything when he saw her. Since her questions continued, he ended the conversation by changing the subject and telling her he wanted her to come by anyway to see her old room, now redone. She finally agreed to be there early with whatever she could find.

With that taken care of, Godfrey settled into bed that night remembering that before installing the molding in the bedroom he intended for Flex, he'd painted the walls. He was especially glad he'd taken on that extra task now, since he recalled they'd previously been pink.

Before long, he contentedly drifted off to sleep with a head and heart full of plans to provide for Flex whatever his worthy young life required.

CHAPTER FIVE

When his daughter arrived the next morning, as promised, with no-longer-needed boy's clothes, Godfrey quickly explained his plans. Despite her apprehension about her father's impulsive intentions, she agreed to his additional request that she call the school board office for complete instructions on school enrollment. He then hugged and thanked her as he hurried her off before she could lecture him further against taking in strangers. She left reluctantly, although very worried, but wished him luck.

The diner was awhirl with customers when Godfrey went in around 7:00. He spied Flex efficiently bussing tables amidst the breakfast-time rush. Since it was obvious Flex wouldn't be available soon, Godfrey used this chance to discuss his plans with Ed.

"Man, I've known you a long time but never thought you'd do anything like this," Ed answered, stunned by the idea. "I assure you though, I want to do what I can to help Flex, if it's only to keep him working here. You know about all the property and money I've had stolen by former employees, and I know Flex can be trusted. Anyway, he really needs a break, and I want to do what I can to help him get one."

They both realized Flex was independent enough to want to feel like he was pulling his own weight, so they agreed on a trial work schedule. Flex could work the 6:00 morning shift until school time and then the supper rush around 4:30. He would stay as long as possible, depending on the amount of homework he'd have each day. With that settled, they agreed that Godfrey would return later that morning to take Flex for a haircut and get him re-registered into school.

When Flex and Godfrey left the diner later, Flex only expected a haircut. He was understandably dumbstruck when Godfrey shocked him with the news that he could stay with him. "I know this is a lot to take in, Flex, but my plan is to get you re-registered into school right away. We'll go get your hair cut first and then I'll bring you to the house for a shower. We'll leave for the school board office as soon as you're ready so we'll get there before they leave for lunch."

On the drive to the barbershop, Flex quietly listened, wide-eyed and unbelieving, as Godfrey explained the importance of education and the necessity for getting him back in school. When exiting the barber chair, Flex immediately grabbed his neck with both hands, stunned at the sight of his reflection, and soon relaxed in admiration of it. There were compliments, along with warnings about girls' advances, from all waiting their turns. A proud, almost stoic Flex returned to Godfrey's truck with erect shoulders that prominently displayed an updated yet not-too-short haircut.

Once in the house, Godfrey led Flex to where clothes were laid out on the bed for him in what was to be his room. The result was an extraordinarily long time of Godfrey convincing Flex it REALLY would be his room and these TRULY would be his clothes. When he assumed he'd been successful, Godfrey went on to explain the diner work schedule he and Ed planned for him, but couldn't continue when he soon realized he had none of Flex's attention.

A stunned ten-year-old former foster kid with no possessions was jutting from one new thing to another, lovingly touching each. He'd glance back at Godfrey, as if to ask 'Is it true?' and Godfrey would nod, as if to answer 'Of course', and Flex would run over and hug him. Godfrey soon decided this was to become a memory he simply needed to witness and cherish, for he'd learned how rare they were. *Nevertheless*, after Flex had gone from wall to wall in his exhibition of sincere appreciation and was starting into a repeat, a wet-eyed Godfrey was compelled to rush a grateful Flex into the shower.

The ride over to the school board office gave Flex a chance to absorb all this exciting news and become sufficiently calm enough to handle class placement testing. Godfrey was somewhat apprehensive, however, about something his daughter had mentioned, the fact that school officials might ask for proof of guardianship in addition to proof of address. There was no need for concern, as it turned out, because the focus seemed to be more on Flex's entering at the start of the term's second nine-week period, which would begin the following week. Flex did well on the tests and was placed in fifth grade again at the same school, and wasn't assigned a bus, since he preferred walking or riding a bike. It wasn't far, except now he'd be walking or riding upriver. After all necessary paperwork was complete, Flex was given teacher names and corresponding classroom numbers, along with the expected list of necessary school supplies.

Godfrey then returned a very different Flex to the diner and bought him lunch, which Flex ate voraciously as he smiled at Godfrey between almost every bite. After enjoying their lunch together, Godfrey reminded Flex to come 'to his new home' after work that evening. Flex beamed as Godfrey gave him a big hug and headed for home.

That afternoon, although Ilana could hear rustling noises inside his house when she knocked on the screen door, Godfrey didn't answer. He was so busily struggling to move furniture around to arrange things more appropriately for Flex, he only noticed her when she called through the window at the side of the house.

Godfrey looked up and immediately beckoned her in. "You're just in time to give me your opinion on my arrangement! Hey, where's Flower?"

"Blossom, Godfrey, not Flower! The vet suggested I leave her with him so they could clean her up and examine her. He thinks she's far along enough that it's best to keep her there for the delivery in case she has trouble."

"Hmph, And are you sure the vet's place will be comfortable enough for Miss Bouquet so she won't be TOO stressed?"

"Yes, Godfrey, she'll be fine. Also, after the birth, while she's there, she'll get her shots and micro chipping."

"You know, I never even gave that dog a bath in all the time she hung around here, so for sure, if you hadn't come along, that micro whatever thing wouldn't have gotten done."

"It's called micro chipping, Godfrey, and it's important enough to be mandatory. You see, a small chip is inserted under an animal's skin. It's scanned, and, by computer, is connected to the owner's complete information. As a result— there are no lost pets!"

"I see. Let me just get this straight right now. That dog will give birth to puppies, then get shots, and then have something put IN HER SKIN? Well, I'm no authority, but I'd think all that happening to her might cause her some stress!"

"Oh, it'll be alright, and, to answer your question, your arrangement looks nice, and I think you've got the lamp situated in a good useful place by the desk and chair. You did good, Godfrey! And, you know what I've decided? If the puppies are girls, I'll call them Violet, Pansy, and Jasmine. Don't know what the names will be if they're boys though. Any ideas?"

"How 'bout Branch or Shrub or Fern or maybe Leaf?" He pulled out a kitchen chair for her and continued, "Hey, I've been busy but I didn't forget you were comin', so I've got the coffee drippin' and cake from the diner."

"That sounds perfect. I had a hectic day at the hospital with hardly a lunch break."

"Now I do want to hear all about you, like I said, but I've got brand new news!" Before Ilana could ask about what, an excited Godfrey was bubbling over with all he knew about a boy who was going to stay with him.

"Well, that's great!" she interjected when he finally paused. "I need to ask though, were there no questions at registration about where Flex lived before and how he came to live with you? Not only am I a parent, Godfrey, but I'm also a retired school music teacher, so I'm somewhat familiar with how things work with the school system."

"You know, my daughter mentioned that too but they didn't ask."

"A likely possibility is the assumption that Flex is another transplanted Katrina victim. Everyone still wants to do whatever possible to make things easier for those kids. You know, Godfrey, it's really wonderful that you're willing to help him like this. You're a very special person."

"Yeah well, don't spread it around! Anyway, he seems like a good kid who had to grow up before he should have, and he could use some kindness. His name's Phillip Foster, by the way, and he's only 10, although he tried to con me into thinking he was 16. I've got two extra bedrooms and, since ones empty, why not? The other one I kinda use for storage, but he'll have the bigger one. I've been fixin' it up for him all afternoon and puttin' away some clothes my daughter brought over for him. When he's done at the diner, he'll walk over here. And, you know what? I can hardly wait for him to get here. But that'll be much later, so I've got plenty time to hear about you. So now, let's hear it!"

"Now Godfrey, you know what? I just might have some games and books and things Flex could use. When I moved, I kept some things that belonged to my kids. I'll see what I can come up with that Flex might like."

"Wonderful! I hadn't thought of that. I was more focused on getting his school supplies in time. Now, I'm ready to hear about you and your life! So shoot!"

"Well," Ilana began warily, "you know I like dogs, and you must think

I'm pretty nosy and maybe a little crazy for coming here that first time. I've just always been fascinated by these properties along the river, so much so that I was drawn here."

"I'm very glad you were drawn here, and I don't think you're TOO nosy. I think you were brave to come. Anyway, how would I have ever gotten rid of that mutt if you hadn't shown up here snoopin' around? Now tell me about what keeps you busy most days and all about your family."

Ilana started by telling him about her volunteer work and how she sincerely loved doing it. "I've also discovered a skill I didn't know I had, Godfrey, that of being able to tactfully handle anxious worried families and friends. I've even been told I make the hospital gift shop a welcoming relief for them—like a desert oasis, away from the suffering and sickness. That makes me really feel good. At the animal shelter, I always seem to be the one wanted to help console pet owners who must put their animals to sleep. But, hey, I don't want you to think its all sadness. I do like my volunteer work, do my best at it, and feel extra lucky that I've the option of choosing to do it."

"I'm so glad for you then. Something I've learned in my many years is how important it is to do what we really enjoy, whether it be as a living or in our free time."

"But, you know, Godfrey, I also get a lot in return too from many thankful people. What's the best is making the children happy and seeing their delighted faces at the shelter when they get to choose a long-awaited pet."

"That's how you know about dogs and the chip thing I guess—from the shelter. Now, tell me about your family. What are they like? I know you have a daughter."

"Yes, Godfrey, her name's Amelie, and I have a son, Addison, who's older. Here are some pictures of them in growing-up stages. He's the solid dependable type and she kind of walks on the wild side. All in all, if I had to describe their personalities, at least when younger, I'd say they seemed to complement each other. He kept her centered and focused and she made sure he had fun." Ilana further elaborated on their careers and how contented they seemed to be in them. She then added how grateful she was for their help and support during her life-changing divorce. "And you know, Godfrey, even though they're always available to me, I'm glad I don't have to contact them anymore because of need. We seem to call each other lately for catching up, and even sometimes, just for laughs. I love them so!"

When Godfrey asked about their father, she told him she and her ex were now on amicable terms, despite his initial defiance at her wanting the divorce. "Godfrey, I know you and your wife were happy together, and I know it takes work, and I tried, really tried, for a long time. But with us, there was no common interest at all. Our preferences, our future plans, and even our natures were completely different. Maybe opposites attract, and it must have worked initially in getting us together, but having absolutely nothing we could agree on made me miserable. I just couldn't see myself in that situation until death, so, to me, divorce was inevitable. But I didn't go into the divorce without a lot of thought. I even tried to analyze my feelings on my own, you know, as if in therapy."

"And did you learn anything?" He seemed intrigued by that statement.

"Not really. I guess I tried to see if I was to blame, so I even went as far as to question myself about other possibilities for my not wanting to be with him. I wondered if I had somehow doomed the marriage. I mean, could I have expected too much from him maybe, by wanting him to measure up to the great opinion I had of my dad?"

"Oh, that's kinda deep—but I guess it's a possibility. Anyway, I truly believe that God wants happiness for all of us, and he provides the opportunities to find it."

Suddenly realizing she had told him things only her children and close friends knew, and somewhat embarrassed at having done so, Ilana exclaimed apologetically, "Oh, now I've gone on way too long with this. You must be especially easy to talk to, Godfrey, for I've not opened up about this in a good while and I'm so sorry to have bored you with it. I've enjoyed the visit and coffee and cake, but I should go."

"Ilana, it could be that you really needed to talk about these things, and I certainly haven't been bored. I've been honored to listen."

"I'll be back with whatever I find that Flex might like, but I want to meet him, so I'll call first to make sure he's here."

Ilana did hug Godfrey before leaving this time—for it seemed so right.

CHAPTER SIX

Blossom had trouble delivering her pups, but ultimately brought into the world a flowery brood of two females and one male. The vet intended to keep them for shots and micro chipping, so Ilana rushed over to see them as soon as she could get away. Amelie saved vacation days for when the pups went home in order to help Ilana get them settled in, so they picked them up together the Friday after the birth. Amelie all along intended to take one of the pups, but after seeing them, naturally wanted them all. Realizing that couldn't happen, she insisted on watching them constantly, while limiting herself to only holding them occasionally.

Although Ilana had chosen names for them, she wanted her daughter's input regarding which name would go with which pup, so over the weekend, names were decided. A tan female became Jasmine; the other female was black enough to appear a deep purple, so she was Violet; and the name, Chicory, seemed to perfectly fit the smallest, a coffee-colored male.

Ilana took advantage of Amelie's being with her for the weekend and dragged her away from the pups long enough to help her find some things for Flex.

"Amelie, you know how I insisted on keeping these games and toys for possible future grandkids to play with...."

"Yes, Mom, and I remember the major challenge it was removing them from a large attic and finding room to store them here in this much smaller place. And now I'm afraid it seems you'd like to move them again. Right?"

"Well, yes, but it seems our efforts to store them are going to prove worthwhile even sooner than I expected. If these things can add more enjoyment to Flex's new life, I'll be so proud to give them to him, and partly because you and Addison took such good care of them. I must say, we have a pretty good collection of books and board games that are in exceptional condition. That's another reason I wanted to save them."

Ilana remembered the many fights that erupted between the siblings at picking-up time. She understood a child's reluctance to putting things where they belonged at the conclusion of a game, but also knew the importance of their getting accustomed to doing it. Squabbles resulted often between her two, but she realized early on they were due to Addison's tendency toward neatness and Amelie's complete lack of patience. Knowing the cause helped her to settle many arguments—though regrettably, not nearly enough.

"I have to say, Mom, it was Addison who pushed me in that taking-care-of-things direction, and I guess I'll have to thank him."

"That would be nice. I know I'll be complimenting him!"

"This old boom box still plays, Mom, but it's so big, Flex might not have room for it." When Amelie plugged it in, turned it on, and found a clear radio station, they decided its great sound was a definite toward its making the cut. "Hey, that little dude will have to find room for this! Of all these things, this might be the most important of them all."

After confirming Sunday afternoon as a good time to see Flex, Ilana and Amelie drove over to Godfrey's to find both he and Flex drinking Pepsis on the back porch of the old house. Ilana brought over a coconut cake she had made, since she now knew it to be Godfrey's favorite. Right there on the old porch, she, Amelie, and Godfrey turned the occasion into a spontaneous welcoming celebration for Flex.

After sensing enough get-acquainted time was spent over more cake and Pepsi, Ilana asked, "Could I get some help from you guys in getting some things from the car?"

"Sure!" Flex answered energetically as he jumped off the porch. "Lead me to 'em!" As soon as the car trunk rose, he exclaimed, "Wow—a boom box! Those are great! I've heard they've got better sound than even the things you put in your ear."

"Well, Mom, what did I tell you? It's a hit!" Amelie squealed.

Flex turned to them quizzically as they said in unison, "IT'S YOURS!"

"All of it!" Ilana added. "In these boxes are books and games that Amelie and her brother had at your age, and we thought you could get some good use out of them."

Flex's young heart had never experienced anything like all this recent kindness, and he blurted out, "Wow! I never played these games or even saw them before, and the books..." Fighting back tears, he hugged and thanked Ilana and Amelie repeatedly.

They brought it all into the house and, of course, found a spot for the boom box. As it played, they helped Flex find appropriate places for the rest of his new things while his small face seemed to glisten in a continuous smile.

In the kitchen later, Godfrey asked, "Say, Ilana, don't you have some new little Geraniums, Daisies, and Petunias by now at your house?"

"Oh, they're the cutest things! Their names are Jasmine, Violet, and Chicory. Flex, we've got new little puppies now at my house and their mama's name is Blossom."

"You know, Ilana," Godfrey interjected, "if you have too many, maybe we could find some extra room here and take one off your hands. That is, if it's okay with Flex."

At that point, Flex could no longer hold back his tears. He hugged Godfrey and sobbed uncontrollably, "Oh, wow, I'll really have a puppy too? I never thought that could ever happen—first you, Godfrey, and then a new place to live, with my own room, and all my new clothes and things, and new friends—and now—even a puppy!"

When she could get him calmed and his attention focused again, Ilana explained that he wouldn't be able to get the pup until it was old enough to no longer need its mother. Although anxious, he understood, and when she and Amelie left, it was with Ilana's promise to bring them over soon for him to choose one.

On the way home, Ilana mentioned, "You know, Amelie, with Flex having a puppy, we'll get to see it often. My hunch is that he'll take Chicory because it's a male."

"Geez, I should make my decision because the pups are going fast, but it's SO hard. Since Violet's been my true favorite all along, I guess she's the one I really want!"

Addison decided, after hearing Flex's story, yet not having met him, that a good bike for riding to school was a necessity. He also figured more current boom box tapes were in order. Since he'd be bringing those over to Godfrey's anyway, he planned an upcoming weekend with his mother when he could help her bring the pups to show Flex.

When that weekend came around and Flex saw the puppies, he had no trouble deciding. Chicory was his immediate choice—not only because he was male, but because he was small. Not right away, but soon, Flex would have a puppy. He also now owned a bike, and that was IMMEDIATE. Although well prepared and anxious for the puppy, he was totally shocked and thrilled with the bike.

Apparently Addison chose the perfect bike and the coolest boom box tapes, for it was apparent to all how impressed Flex was with Addison. Upon closer scrutiny though, one would realize Addison didn't rank high on Flex's admiration scale because of those things. Of all the new friends he'd recently met, Flex somehow knew he'd found a very special one in Addison.

The following weeks had Ilana's attention almost completely focused on puppy well-being, which meant her going home to check on them daily and requesting fill-in from other volunteers so she could leave early. She was embarrassed to solicit the help of neighbors she had only spoken to briefly during her move into the complex. But, apparent animal lovers, they gladly helped out. Getting to know them reconfirmed to Illana that she'd made the right townhouse choice. Amelie came often to help, and Addison made repeated trips to assist with puppy paper-training and dog discipline. His coming so often surprised her more, since he lived farther away.

The eight-week period went smoothly, except for the unavoidable frustration involved in house training and the expected predicaments the pups managed to get into. Jasmine was the pup usually in trouble, thus the need for almost constant watching. Ilana stayed in contact with Godfrey and Flex only by phone during that time, for Flex called often to check on Chicory. She came to cherish those conversations, not only because of his updates on his new evolving world, but because they gave her opportunities to offer him additional guidance.

When weeks of caring for those furry energy puffs ended, Ilana felt the inevitable expected anguish involved in parting with Violet and Chicory. She also missed having Amelie and Addison over as frequently and seeing her neighbors regularly. *Nevertheless*, it was comforting to know that puppy training had advanced enough so Amelie and Flex should have little trouble with Violet and Chicory.

Blossom seemed to adjust easily to the absence of her babies. Ilana took their absence much harder, although she couldn't help notice the obvious, how much cleaner and quieter the townhouse was with this new arrangement.

Everything was going well in all their lives until All Saints Day when Godfrey called Ilana to say that Flex had returned from the diner in an uncharacteristically tense mood but wouldn't say what troubled him. He'd said the previous Halloween night was the best he'd ever had and was his usual happy self that morning, but since returning from the diner earlier, he was anxious, and even seemed frightened.

Ilana immediately contacted Addison, since he'd be the best one to reach out to Flex. It was a work holiday for him, so he agreed to drive to Godfrey's that afternoon to talk to Flex, and, the whole drive there, he wished he had more information.

When Addison arrived at Godfrey's and while they awaited Flex's return from his usual sitting-on-the-levee-time, Godfrey told Addison all he knew. They watched from Godfrey's window as Flex soon crossed River Road with head downcast—until he spotted Addison's car. Flex looked up hopefully and immediately began running toward the house. Addison instinctively left Godfrey and ran to meet him. Godfrey watched as Addison lifted Flex up, spun him around, lowered him to the ground, spoke to him a while, and then led him to the old back porch.

After careful questioning, while trying to avoid prying, Addison discovered that Flex was terrified of returning to the diner for a reason he wouldn't disclose. Insisting he didn't want to bother anyone with it, yet reluctant to enlighten Addison as to what IT was, Flex did agree to have Addison accompany him to the diner when he had to return. Since it was a school holiday, Ed wanted Flex to help during meal rush times, so he expected Flex back at the diner around 5:00. This meant there'd be a few awkward hours spent with a clueless and extremely worried Godfrey.

Flex spent the time silently playing with Chicory and hugging him almost constantly, while Addison quietly assured Godfrey he'd do all he could to correct the problem. Although Godfrey suspected Flex was crying, he asked nothing when Flex hugged him an extra long time before he and Addison left.

As they walked over to the diner, Addison made hopeful attempts at light conversation with such questions as: "Must be nice to be off of school for a day?" and "How great was last night's trick-or-treating?" With no response from Flex, who continuously looked down unhappily, Addison opted for silence.

When they got close enough to the diner for Flex to spy a dented and unpainted van parked outside, he suddenly stopped walking and refused to go any farther. He remained still a while, then began turning his head in all directions as if in a panic, and abruptly took off running, Addison close behind him. The fear in Flex's young heart apparently prevented his brain from pointing in the right direction, for he headed toward the woods behind the diner. When he realized he'd ended up at the end of the cleared property and was amid trees on all sides that prevented his advancing, he sank to his knees in hysterical sobs. Addison wished he knew how to comfort away Flex's agony, but all he could do was to sit beside him and hold the small trembling body close to him.

"It's all gonna go away," Flex screamed. "It's all gonna be gone."

"What's going away? What's bothering you? Tell me so I can help you, please."

"They're gonna ruin it all. They're in there waitin' to mess everything up."

"Who do you mean? Is it whoever came in the van? Is that the problem?"

Flex struggled to answer between sobs, "Yeah, I saw 'em drive away in it before."

"Flex, Buddy, talk to me! Who are they?" Addison pleaded. "Who's in the diner now that you don't want to see? Tell me! Who or what are you afraid of?"

"The kids, the kids—I know they came back here to make me go back—the kids from the home, I don't see 'em in school this year so I thought they were somewhere else, but this mornin' they saw me in the diner. I know they'll ruin everything!"

"No, no, no! We won't let them ruin ANYTHING!"

"Please—let me run away where they can't find me," Flex begged through sobs. "I can't let them see me again!"

"No, of course I won't let you run away. I don't quite know what to do, but we'll figure it out. Let me think." After a pause, Addison lifted Flex's chin toward him and continued, "If they're in the diner again because they saw you there and you don't go in there now, they'll just come back when you ARE there. We have to face them, and it might as well be now. We'll go in there together and get it over with. I'll be beside you!" He then added in a feeble attempt at humor to get Flex to relax, "And, hey, I'm a fairly big guy, right? Anyway, I'm sure Godfrey would do anything to keep you here no matter what. And Chicory, well Chicory just has to have you with him too. We all love you and want you here forever, so none of us—Godfrey, my mom, my sister, Ed—none of us would let you leave here. Now, let's get you calmed down. Here, use my handkerchief."

"You're really sure about all that?" Flex asked hopefully while wiping his face.

"Absolutely! No question about it! But, we MUST face these kids—now or later! So, listen up! And remember now! I'm right by your side! Are you ready? At Flex's tentative nod and tight squeeze of Addison's hand, Addison said softly, yet emphatically, "Okay...Now...WE'RE GOING IN!"

CHAPTER SEVEN

As they entered the diner, Addison taking the lead with Flex huddled behind him, a girl came out of the restroom and walked over to them, eyeing Flex carefully. She then walked to a booth and said something to the group seated there, and a tall kid came toward Flex saying, "It is the Flexer! We weren't sure it was you. We had a bet goin'."

"Yeah, then I win!" came another voice from the booth as the boy stood up saying, "Man, ya clean up good."

Another came over and said, "Ya buffed up some since I saw ya. Ya must be eatin' good, huh, man? You eat here?"

The girl pointed her finger at Flex, saying, "You know I saw you in school a couple times and only knew you looked familiar. Guess it's the haircut and the nice duds that fit on that filled out bod of yours. You're lookin' good, Flexer. And who's the guy?"

"This is Addison," Flex answered shyly.

The last kids still in the booth walked over and one said, "We snuck off with my buddy with the wheels here. He was gonna take us to New Orleans since there wasn't any school, you know because of All Saints Day, but the old heep only made it this far this mornin'. Then once we saw you, we had to come back when he got the car fixed so we could check out for sure if it WAS you." As he circled Flex closer, he added, "Lookin' good lil man. Show me some flexin'," to which Flex exposed an arm muscle.

The others laughed and chimed in with "Man, I love it!" and "Lookin' good!" and "Good to see ya," at which point Flex seemed to relax somewhat. Then someone shouted out, "Lil man, we're proud a ya for checkin' outta that place, no matter how you did it. I sure wish I had a place to run away to."

From the girl came, "Good for you, Flexer. You got some guts. You know that?"

And Flex, with a baffled expression, said "But you guys were so mean to me."

"Nah, we were just buggin' ya and gettin a kick out of it 'cause you used to try so hard to get back at us," one of the boys said as he grabbed Flex affectionately around the shoulders. "Hey, we had to get our laughs somehow!"

"Say, how long you been gone?" one asked. "Nobody over there has noticed we're one less in the house. Gosh, I sure wish I could leave."

"Hey, we all can't start leavin'," another said. "They'd begin to notice somethin' different. Well maybe after a while, they would. Ya know, we musta' treated ya bad, I gotta say, but hey, I guess we had to pick on somebody. Sorry, lil dude! But how tough was it to just up and leave? How did ya even get away?"

"Yeah, lil dude, how'd that go down?" came this and similar questions from all of them, now all at the same time, as they led Flex toward their booth.

And so, with Addison's prodding, Flex proceeded to tell them when and how he'd left. After a while he began to really loosen up and even laugh with them. At that point Addison walked over to Ed, who had been watching it all. Before Ed could question him, Addison said, "Ed, I'm sorry about this. I know he should be working, but could you give him some time with them? I think this is really important."

"Oh, it's okay, really! Not many customers today. Everyone's at the cemeteries I guess, cleaning graves, and maybe brought their lunches. But can you let me in on what's goin' on? These kids were in here this mornin' and Flex ducked out as soon as he spotted 'em. I worried about why he left, but was too busy to call Godfrey."

Addison went on to tell him who it seemed these kids were and that apparently Flex had been afraid of their seeing him because he feared they'd shatter his new life. As it turned out, in the past these kids were only blowing off steam and taking their frustrations out on Flex—and maybe to the extreme, from Flex's point of view. *Nevertheless,* they weren't bad kids—just very unhappy ones.

"What a great ending for the little fella after dreading seeing them," Ed responded. "You know, Addison, I did worry some that there might be a question about his change of address when Godfrey registered him into school, but maybe it didn't seem out of the ordinary with all the students resettling into different schools after Katrina."

"Yes, I know. All the schools around here have done everything possible to accommodate kids from New Orleans and Chalmette, so registering Flex, as it turned out, didn't bring up any questions."

When Addison glanced over at them in the booth, Flex anxiously waved him over, saying, "Addison, come tell them about Chicory. Don't I have a puppy! Tell them."

"Yeah, Ad, I can hardly believe the good life he's into now," one said as Addison joined them, "and a puppy too? Aw, no—I can't believe that," he said, smiling at Flex.

So Addison, with his arm around Flex, elaborated on Chicory and what Flex had told them. "Yep, we've all come to love this little guy—maybe especially Chicory."

"We all love him too, down deep" one answered. "You know, we're the ones who gave him his name. Matter of fact, I don't even know the Flexer's real name."

"For your information, it's Phillip Foster," Flex exclaimed proudly.

"Well I need to know how he came to be called Flex," Addison inquired.

One of them explained, "Aw, he wanted to show off by tryin' to flex a muscle, but he had trouble findin' a muscle somewhere in them scrawny arms, so we started calling him "The Flexer.""

"Yeah," another said, "then it automatically got shortened to Flex. I guess we did ride you pretty hard, lil man, now that I think about it. Sorry 'bout that."

And they all echoed the sentiment, some grabbing Flex's hand across the booth, those closer squeezing his shoulders as they said, "Yeah, sorry, man."

"Well, how about I get you kids something to eat? I'm buyin'!" Addison said, as everyone stared at him with mouths dropped open.

"Oh, really?" the girl asked. "That'd wonderful! Oh, and he's good lookin' too!"

"Would you all like hamburgers and fries or a hot plate or just a dessert?" Addison asked as he looked around at their unbelieving faces and reinforced the offer. "Really—my treat! I'll get a waitress and you all order whatever you want," and he went to summon someone willing to handle this group of eight, including Flex and himself.

"You know, Flex, me and Henry are fixin' ta get in shop class next year and learn somethin' about fixin stuff," Addison heard one kid say as he walked away. It was like he was talking to a real pal, and continued on, "We figure when we get outta school, a job'll be much easier to get. Well, we're really hopin' it'll happen anyway."

And the conversations continued while they waited for the order, conversations between friends, friends who knew they'd each been through heartaches. A reason or opportunity to discuss their pasts probably never came up and possibly never would, yet their mutual anguish had given them a bond they all fully understood. The meal they awaited might be their first good meal in memory. When it came, they especially relished it, not only for its culinary goodness, or more importantly perhaps because it was free, but because they were enjoying it together.

Addison later drew Flex to the side to make sure he'd be comfortable with his leaving for his long return drive home. Flex's expression said it all, for he was beaming. To have gone from the total fear he felt only a few hours ago to this elation at being accepted, and even admired, was obviously a major self-affirming turnaround for him. Addison left to report to Godfrey on the happenings of the past few hours and then called his mother with the good news. He soon headed home, thinking all was right with the world.

CHAPTER EIGHT

All was right with the world also from the perspective of a wealthy New Orleans gentleman of distinction. From his impressive home in the New Orleans Faubourg (suburb) Marigny, Tarlton Daunois drove onto the ferry that crossed the mighty Mississippi River, the entrance into the Heartland. Although there were bridges in any direction convenient to him, Tarlton always preferred the ferry ride so he could be closer to the river, a sensation he'd enjoyed since childhood, that of being almost in it rather than above it.

He leaned over the ferry railing and watched the murky water as he and other passengers shared pleasantries while enjoying the sunny breeze. Being able to enjoy a ferry ride while standing outside a car—even in December—was just one of the many things about New Orleans this thankful citizen treasured. Tarlton was a native New Orleanian, his family having lived there for many generations, so he was well aware of the progress commerce on the river brought to the city. Throughout New Orleans history, it created on-going jobs that gave the city endurance and stability, an ironic contrast, he thought while looking down, to the turbulence the circling eddies caused on the river's surface.

Having been an only child had afforded Tarlton the luxury of being the sole heir to his family's assets, and, although his wealth was initially inherited, he'd invested it wisely during the ensuing years. Though an extremely generous benefactor, his humility demanded that his charitable donations be handled quietly. His monetary gifts were made solely in an effort to help someone or to correct a wrong—not so they'd be tax write-offs.

An enthusiastic Tarlton was on his way to Riverside on this sunny afternoon, for he was finally about to bring his long-thought-out idea into the open. He was to present to their parish officials a plan he felt could help many people. He was inspired by a serious problem he saw developing in many areas and hadn't allowed anything to dissuade his doing what he could to correct it. Typical of all his endeavors, he'd spent months studying his project's possibilities, doing thorough research, and then seeking its appropriate location. Ultimately, he designated Riverside as, not only the perfect place, but the only place acceptable. The opportunity of finally sharing his plan with those who could allow him to actually make it happen was just ahead. In the past, he'd made substantial contributions to other areas around New Orleans and sincerely hoped to begin to also do as much for Riverside.

Arriving at the parish courthouse earlier than he expected, he decided this extra time was a good opportunity to call his daughter, the most important person in his life. Both their schedules left them little time for seeing each other, so he jumped at this chance to possibly catch her when she was able to talk a while.

"Dad," she answered, seeing her phone caller identification. "Hi, where are you?"

"Oh, in Riverside about to go into the meeting I've been waiting for. And, sweetie, if it goes well, let's get together so I can tell you the results. Okay?"

"Sure! Just say when," she answered enthusiastically.

"Great! Now, is everything going okay in your world?"

"Oh sure, Dad. Pretty much the usual with me—about to complete a project now, and then I'm on to another. Say, why don't we meet for dinner tonight? After all, what you've told me of your project sounds wonderful, and you'd be the one to pull it off, so I don't have a doubt in the world that it'll go well."

"I'd love for us to have dinner tonight, and I hope your confidence in me is on the mark! I'll call you later to set up a time and place. And it's my treat!"

"Sounds like a winner, and now it looks like I've got another call. So gotta run. Love you and see you later. Bye."

"Bye, my darling, and I love you too." He hung up from someone he thought the world of, and for whom he was eternally grateful. She was the only result of two failed marriages—his pride, his Marvel. It was her name, yet could accurately describe her. She was smart, upbeat, pretty, competent at whatever interested her AND unattached. It constantly amazed him that no guy had yet come along who could sway her heart into marriage, but at 26, she was very happy with her independence. They discussed her being single whenever he brought it up, and it always ended the same way: by her challenging him with the fact that he himself was also unattached. In addition to his marriages, there had been many shallow relationships that he soon discovered were rooted in greed, so he was now as content in his freedom as Marvel was in hers.

After checking the time and gathering his things from the car, he approached the building and headed toward the designated meeting room. Heads turned as he walked through the lobby while he smiled a good afternoon to those who met his glance. He was closing in on sixty and had some gray hair that proved it, but he had a charm that made him handsome by putting him in control. He usually dressed casually, but his straight, upright physique gave him an admirable air of superiority, in whatever he wore.

When he entered the meeting room, all heads turned. Though no one recognized him, all were impressed. Everyone in New Orleans would know him, but he wasn't familiar around here, where everyone knew everyone else, or at least knew someone in their family. Daunois wasn't even a familiar name to anyone in attendance. *Nevertheless,* he had gotten their attention simply by arriving.

A man introducing himself as the parish president walked over and shook Tarlton's hand while leading him to a chair at the head of a large oval table. Around the table were possibly every available parish dignitary. Chairs were moved around and papers shuffled as they all found places. An opening prayer was said with all answering 'Amen,' after which the president made the introductions and turned the floor over to Tarlton, while all the others took their seats.

"Well, thank you, sir," Tarlton began, "and I'm extremely pleased to meet you all. So as not to take up much of your valuable time, I'll get right to what I've got in mind. In a nutshell, it's a project that will accommodate people needing assistance, but not of the usual financial kind. It's an inter-generational living arrangement all under one roof, with a room and bath for each resident. It would be a place where older people teach skills and baby-sit for those who're working or in training. They, in turn, would reciprocate with household chores, chauffeuring, and running errands. There are parents needing baby sitters when they're working, while very lonely, yet capable, older citizens are willing to fulfill those baby-sitting duties but don't have the stamina to do it alone full time. Older people could assist in cooking or vegetable-planting while teaching life lessons.

"My major concern, however, is for the adolescents needing structure. Their daily home life doesn't provide it, for various and sometimes unavoidable reasons. They're good kids who quickly get lured into crime as an easier way to achieve the funds they'd like for the fun things in life they deserve in their youth.

"Regrettably, the economy has caused such downsizing that homelessness is almost inevitable because competent carpenters, artists, landscapers, seamstresses, musicians, and so many others can't find work. You might even know people who are eager to learn a trade and some who have talents and would be willing to teach them. What's needed is coordination of the needs with the availabilities.

"Your public transportation gets people with visual and age-related impairments to necessary appointments, but my plan would allow them to also visit friends. Some older people tend to avoid inconveniencing others, but this endeavor would keep them from feeling like an imposition since they'd know they were reciprocating. Loneliness can easily lead to mental and physical illnesses. Many enter nursing homes merely because they don't want to be, or shouldn't be, living alone. I see an urgent necessity for this project because minds crave activity and interaction, and available skills aren't being utilized.

"You'll find my specific plan of action, along with my research, in these copies I'm handing out for you to review. I've known of this need for a long time and am now convinced this is the appropriate place. My reasons for choosing Riverside, by the way, are: its proximity to a bridge over the river, its transportation system, a state-of-the-art hospital with its adjunct clinics, and an efficient and successfully-run sheriff's office.

"Now, regarding your involvement, I've saved the best for last. Normally this type venture would necessitate acquiring grants, however my lucrative investments allow me to completely fund it in the beginning. Once established, it could soon result in being completely self-sufficient. The cooperation of all your departments will be needed for the success of this endeavor, however, so I'd appreciate it, along with your input. If there are no questions, that concludes my presentation and I'll let you get back to your work."

As there was no discussion, yet all seemed interested, the parish president stood to say, "Well, Mr. Daunois, this seems most interesting, yet very surprising to me that no one has proposed such an idea already."

His statement was accompanied by nods of agreement from the others as he continued, "I'm very pleased you've chosen Riverside and I'm sure those in attendance are enthused enough as well to offer our full cooperation. We can look it over now if you like, or we can let you know after giving it some time. I am curious as to what exact land location you've got in mind though."

"That's not definite at this point because of the amount of land it would require, so I'd be interested in any real estate listings I'm not aware of that you'd deem appropriate. You know where to reach me, so call or e-mail your input or questions, and please contact me or my lawyer with your decision—fairly soon though, because time, energy, and ability are being wasted. I thank you all for your time." After some applause, the group gathered around Tarlton to shake his hand and extend their good wishes. Someone brought in coffee and they socialized a while; and then a very pleased Tarlton Daunois made his exit, feeling extremely encouraged by their reactions.

He drove out of the courthouse parking lot toward the river, but instead of turning onto the bridge ramp entrance, he enjoyed his ride on River Road so completely that he continued on farther to absorb the sights, sounds and smells of the landscape. The gold-green levee grass had been freshly mowed, so the egrets were discovering their eating treasures in the shorter lawn. Bike-riders were atop the levee with dogs running alongside and joggers could be seen farther away downriver. Seriously wanting to climb over the levee to sit and watch the river, Tarlton looked for a flat surface on the levee side of the road to pull the car over.

After traveling about a mile before finding a spot, he parked, grabbed a bottle of water, and started to run up the levee. After only a few steps, he realized he no longer could do things that came automatically in the past, so then commenced to slowly ascend the levee. He heard a ship's horn as he reached the top and saw by the logo and location on its side how astonishingly far the ship had come. The distances ships traveled to transport things always fascinated Tarlton. Wanting to sit and watch a while, he began looking for a rock to sit on that was lower and closer to the river.

He noticed someone sitting almost at the water's edge and walked over in that direction, all the while recalling how much easier it was to walk down the levee. He managed to find a boulder behind what he realized was a young boy who was sitting very close to the water. Tarlton was somewhat concerned for the boy's safety and careful not to startle him. He must have been completely enthralled by the intrigue of the river, for he failed to notice Tarlton behind him.

After a while, Tarlton asked, "Isn't it great to sit out here and watch?"

The boy jumped up and started to leave, saying, "I didn't know anyone was here."

"That's probably because you're as amazed as I am by it all. You don't have to leave. I'll sit here and be quiet if you like."

"Oh but I do have to go!"

"But I've got some questions that maybe a thoughtful guy like you could answer."

"Mister, you look like somebody who's got all the answers. I gotta go."

"No, please, where are you rushing off to? I'm harmless, really, just new to this area and have some questions and could use some suggestions."

"Mister, they'll be looking for me to help with the supper crowd at the diner."

"Oh, where's that? You mean that place across the road over there?" Tarlton asked, pointing. "Hey, is the food good there? See? I need you to suggest a place to eat."

"Oh yeah, its got good food! It's a great place, and I help it to be that way," the boy said proudly.

"Oh? Wonderful! Then I won't keep you. They must need you there right now."

"Yeah, they sure do! Hey, you can stop in there to eat sometime maybe. See ya."

"I'll do that—maybe soon. So long!"

Tarlton watched the boy run up the levee and disappear on the other side. He then took out his Blackberry and jotted a note to himself to eat at Ed's Diner the next time he was on this side of the river. After absorbing the view a while longer and finishing his water, he got in his car and drove toward the ferry for home, where he made a K-Pauls reservation for that night to have dinner with his lovely daughter.

CHAPTER NINE

Early the following week, Tarlton answered the phone to hear his lawyer exclaim, "It's a go! Riverside parish officials have approved your project, so it can happen as soon as you decide on a location. After some cheering and congratulating, Tarlton hung up and contacted the real estate agent who was to help him find an available land site. He purposely set up a meeting with her on the same weekday that he had seen the interesting kid sitting by the river before. He also planned the tour of available properties to be completed by the approximate time he remembered the kid being on the levee that day.

Since the properties large enough for Tarlton's project were limited, the afternoon tour of the few appropriate ones didn't take long. With no real prospect for a location, when he and the real estate agent parted, he was very discouraged. *Nevertheless,* he knew he might be overly anxious for the perfect place to immediately materialize. He tended toward impatience normally, so he tried his best to remain hopeful. After all, the parish officials might even come up with something, since they were so enthusiastic about having it in their parish.

Tarlton drove along the river and found the same parking spot beside the levee as he'd used before. He grabbed his bottle of water, left the car, and this time climbed up the levee at more of a walking pace. He located the same rock he'd sat on and positioned himself comfortably on it to enjoy the river. Before long, he heard the grass rustle as a bike approached from his left. He turned to find the same boy from before dropping his backpack to the ground.

"Hi Mister. You here again, huh?"

"Yes! Hi! It's good to see you. I met someone here in Riverside earlier, so decided to sit up here a while and watch the barges and boats on the river. It's all so fascinating!"

"Oh, yeah! I love it here. My favorite thing is listening to the tugboat captains early in the morning. They can push those heavy barges so far. I like how the empty barges sit up high in the water, and then how low down the filled ones can get."

"Now, you know, not everyone notices that. I sure like your style, little guy. I'm Tarlton Daunois, and I'm very glad we've crossed paths."

"Thank you, sir. I'm Flex Foster and it's nice to meet you," Flex answered as he extended his hand to shake hands with Tarlton and then sat on a rock close by.

"Aren't there school busses around here?" Tarlton asked. "There must be."

"Oh sure, but I don't ride the bus. I rather walk on the levee. I either walk or ride my bike—both ways every day—even when it's cold or raining."

"So you're really an outdoor kinda guy then?"

"Yeah, I guess I am. You comin' to the diner?"

"As a matter of fact, I'd like to. Are you going there now right from school?"

"No. Sometimes I do, but I usually go home first because I'm usually hungry."

"Oh, your mom will have a snack ready for you, huh?"

"It's the most wonderful person in the world who'll have somethin' ready for me. His name's Godfrey—but I call him God for short—because he is to me."

Stunned by this response, yet so impressed, Tarlton started to ask more but quickly reconsidered, thinking he was still too much of a stranger, and only said, "If I ever get to meet him, I know I'd surely like his style too."

"Yeah, he's pretty special. He's old I guess, but he still does stuff."

"Does he go to the diner sometime?"

"Sometimes he goes there for supper if he's been busy with somethin' all day and didn't cook anything, but I know tonight he was cookin' spaghetti. That's my favorite!"

"Mine too! I was thinking about having dinner at the diner later. Say, maybe I could treat you and Godfrey to some dessert later. What do you think?"

"If he's not watchin' the news or some western movie, he'll come," Flex answered excitedly. "And he'll come for coconut cake!"

"Good, I may see you both there later then."

"Okay, see ya," Flex called out as he ran off up the levee.

Tarlton got Marvel on the phone as he watched a plane soar higher and higher through the blue above him. "By any chance, are you free right after work, Sweetie? Your old dad has found a great little place in Riverside where I'll be for a while. Any chance you'd like to cross the river and join me for an early dinner here while it's still daylight? You said you'd like to see more of the area I've been telling you about."

"Well, you know, I'm accustomed to my escorts coming to get me, but I'll make this exception since it's a wonderful reason not to go exercise at the gym."

"Great! Let me tell you where it is." And they proceeded to set up a time and he supplied directions. Since she told him when she'd be leaving work, he could predict her time of arrival, for he knew the shortcuts she'd take and also how fast she usually drove. While he waited and enjoyed the cool breezes, he thought of something that would really please Flex. He had some acquaintances who might know a tugboat captain or two. How thrilled Flex would be if he could spend some time with one!

By the time Marvel arrived, her dad was settling into a booth at the diner and ordering them some wine. She kissed him on the cheek while chattering about how she should be at the mall getting Christmas gifts and sat across the booth from him.

"Right on time, Sweetie," Tarlton greeted her while grabbing her hand. "And come on, you know you're going to order all your gifts on-line like always anyway."

"You know me so well," she laughed, "and how'd you spot this place?"

"Well, I guess I found it because of my love for the old muddy Mississippi," and he went on to bring her up to date on his failure to find a location and his meeting Flex and also of his hope that Flex and his friend, Godfrey, would join them later.

Marvel listened with some concern about location, for she knew how hopeful her father was to begin fulfilling his dream. He soon pointed out to her a very busy Flex, who stopped bussing tables long enough to come over and say that Godfrey would be coming.

"Nice to meet you, Marvel," Flex responded when Tarlton introduced him to her. Then he said to Tarlton, "Oh, Mr. Daunois, I'm so glad to hear she's your daughter because I was thinkin' she was WAY too young for ya," as Tarlton laughed loudly.

"It's a pleasure to meet you, Flex," Marvel chuckled. "I'm looking forward to meeting Godfrey too."

When Godfrey came in, Flex noticed how nice he looked in gray shirt and pants instead of in khakis. Flex left his tray to meet him and introduce him to his new friends, planning to finish up quickly so he could join them.

Tarlton ordered them coconut cake and coffee, and Flex soon came over and sat down with them as Tarlton was explaining his reason for being in Riverside.

"Yes, I'm so hoping to make a go of this in what I consider the perfect place," Tarlton continued. "So, Godfrey, how'd you come to live here originally."

"Well, maybe in the best way—I was born here, spent my youth here, and then traveled a lot when I worked on a crew that built service stations." He told them how his wife loved the river and of the many hours they spent sitting atop the levee together when they were 'courtin'. By the time they were discussing marriage, it was agreed they could do no better than to raise their children right there in Riverside.

"I've never felt the urge to leave, because everything we needed was here, so I guess I don't understand why my friends want me to travel. It seems to me if you're really content with where you are and what you have, you wouldn't want to go anywhere else."

"Well, Godfrey, then I guess you're the perfect example of a home body," Tarlton answered, "and there's a lot to be said for that. I know I love New Orleans so much that I don't long to go other places"

"I might have the wrong idea, but I always feel that people who travel aren't quite satisfied and are lookin' for somethin'."

"That could very well be," Marvel chimed in. "I'd never thought of it that way, but you might be on to something. Although, it might have to do with the extent someone was forced to travel in their career before they have the option of settling down."

When Flex asked for a second slice of cake and Marvel declined her dad's 'seconds' offer, Flex explained, "I'm only used to eating more because at home, if I don't eat everything, Godfrey gives the rest to Chicory, our dog, and he shouldn't."

"Great name—Chicory!" Marvel exclaimed, "I know it's not a good idea to give dogs table food, but if I had a dog, I'd do it too because I couldn't resist. I love dogs!"

"Yeah," Godfrey chimed in apologetically, "I know I shouldn't give him anything but dog food, but it's automatic. I gave that dog's mother whatever I left for so long, that I guess it's a habit I really should break."

"Godfrey," Tarlton interjected, "Flex pointed out your house to me earlier. Am I right in thinking, because you did construction, that you built that house?"

"Actually my Dad and I did. And I just about rebuilt it over the years. I installed new windows, made closeable shutters, retiled, repainted, and even put a new roof on, with help."

"Say, Marvel," Flex said, after having been in deep thought, "I know where you could get a dog, a real good one, if you want one. She's Chicory's sister."

"Oh but, Flex," Godfrey cautioned, "I'm not sure Ilana could part with Geranium or Petunia or whatever her name is".

"Her name's Jasmine, God," Flex corrected. "I guess you're right, but, Marvel, if you'd see her or Chicory, you'd love them, and their other sister, Violet, too."

"What kind of dogs are they?" Marvel asked, obviously intrigued.

"Oh, we don't know," Flex answered, "but they're great!"

"Well, maybe by now Ilana or Amelie might know what they are, Flex," Godfrey said, and then explained to Tarlton and Marvel, "Amelie is the daughter of our friend, Ilana, and one of the puppies is now Amelie's. Ilana has the mother and the last puppy."

"After I finish my cake, you both can come see Chicory. Okay?" Flex asked.

"Well, sure, if you'd like," Marvel answered, while getting a nod from her father. "Not for long though, Dad was going to show me around Riverside."

"Okay, I'm done," Flex announced as he suddenly stood up. "I'm anxious to see Chicory anyway. I always am!" He hurriedly led the way out the diner and into approaching dusk, with Tarlton struggling to catch up, after hurriedly paying the tab and tip.

When Godfrey unlocked the house door, Chicory was immediately close to Flex, as Marvel exclaimed while petting him, "He's precious. He looks like a small Labrador."

"Please, have a seat," Godfrey said, leading them to chairs."

When Flex seemed to linger with them, Godfrey turned to him to say, "and Flex, don't forget about homework!"

"I've got some I didn't finish, but, Marvel, Chicory will follow me when I go to the bedroom to do it, so you better get a good look at him now."

"Well, just tell me about the girl dog that's available," Marvel said as she pet Chicory—"that is, if she's available."

"She's just like Chicory but blonde, and she's the one that got into the most trouble when they were puppies," Flex laughed. "Maybe Ilana would bring her over."

"Why don't we first find out if she would even let Daffodil go and, if so, then we could contact Marvel?" Godfrey answered.

"Yes, and anyway I'd like to think about actually having a dog first," Marvel confessed. "I'd love it I'm sure, but haven't ever gotten serious about having one again after losing the one we had when I lived at home with Dad."

"Okay," but I know if Ilana can part with her, you'll love Jasmine and she'll love you," Flex said, and then, while looking at Godfrey, "Her name's Jasmine, God."

After Flex went into his room, Godfrey poured them all a glass of cherry bounce, a homemade concoction made with almost any fruit, and, some opine is superior to commercial wine. As they savored its mellow flavor, Marvel asked Godfrey about Riverside, "that is if you don't mind or think I ask too many questions. Dad planned to show me around, but it's even better to hear about it from someone who's lived here."

Godfrey beamed a proud smile and replied, "I don't mind at all telling you everything I know. And you don't ask too many questions, because if there's somethin' you ask that I don't want you to know, you're just not gonna hear it. Anyway, I'm enjoying the company. And then I'd like to hear more about y'all and your lives in New Orleans, and if you don't want to tell me everything, that's fair enough too."

After Godfrey had sufficiently related a short history of Riverside since he first knew it and up to the present with Flex, he continued on about Flex. "You know, I never had a son, only two daughters. Now, our girls hung out in the kitchen and garden with my wife and I and helped out, but for fishin', they didn't care so much. Oh, they both went with me some, but I had to bait their hooks and take off the few fish they caught. Then when my grandsons came along, they'd go—until they got interested in girls. Now with Flex, every time we have a chance, we get in the truck and head out to do some bayou and lake fishin' in my old boat he and I fixed up. I only wish we had the same woods behind us as years ago when I was huntin' and trappin'. There was a pond all the kids around here used to love too, but that became part of the water diversion system. We do get to pick blackberries along the railroad track. That's what I made that bounce out of."

"And it might be the best I've had, Godfrey," Tarlton responded, "I'd better not have any more though. Now, what about Flex? He's a great kid! He's your grandson?"

"Oh no, although I'm sure people assume that—people who don't know me. It's probably easier if they think that." Godfrey went on to explain how Flex came to be with him and elaborated, "Flex told me he got himself into some trouble when trying to escape from foster homes, and really paid for it. And you know, I think it's made him just about fearless. That kid will try to climb anything and crawl under anything and even jump over things that seem higher than him. And you know what's great about it? He's pretty successful at whatever he tries. I just love that lil sucker! Ed says he's a great lil worker too. He helps me out a lot too. Now, your turn! I'll get us some more cherry bounce and you can tell me all about you two—what y'all like to do in New Orleans."

"Godfrey, I'm sure we'd both love it, but I promised Marvel I'd show her around Riverside, if it's not too dark already. It probably is, but we really should go anyway. The next time my real estate agent has property over here to show me, I'll give you a call, and maybe Marvel can join us."

"Yes, and Godfrey," Marvel added, "hold off on asking Ilana about the pup until I can think about it and am sure about it."

"Okay, that's fine. And you can come by anytime. Y'all really don't' even hafta call me ahead when you're comin', except I'd probably be cleaner and look nicer when you'd see me, if you did."

CHAPTER TEN

In only a few days, Tarlton was to be disappointed by what was available in land for his project. The real estate agent found only a few, but they were far too narrow to accommodate the amount of footage Tarlton needed. He couldn't understand why she even bothered showing them to him. Though it was becoming obvious there wasn't anything suitable, he forced himself to remain optimistic.

A pre-scheduled dinner get-together with Godfrey and Flex served to cheer him up somewhat, for Marvel was able to meet them at the diner after work. She came in giving Godfrey the okay to call Ilana about the puppy after deciding she was definitely interested. Tarlton treated them to dinner, after which he apologized if he'd been bad company and confessed his reason: that the property search today had been futile and a complete waste of time. They waited for Flex to finish work, then all left for Godfrey's as before, with Godfrey's promise that cherry bounce would help Tarlton's mood. As they settled in on Godfrey's carport and Flex went to his room, Godfrey proceeded to ask Tarlton to fill him in as promised, "Now, Tarlton, or maybe Marvel can answer this, here you are with this wonderful idea for the good of so many, and where does such a wanting to help come from? I'm curious about where you get that desire?"

"Well, Godfrey, I'm a lucky guy with a very comfortable life in New Orleans—the greatest city ever. Hey, I'm lucky enough to be sitting here sipping your wonderful cherry bounce with excellent company in the quiet southern evening breeze."

"Tell me how you got so lucky, and I'll give you even more cherry bounce."

"Okay, okay! "First of all, Godfrey, I've been fortunate enough to have gotten an education that's enabled me to handle whatever my current challenge has been. And what I didn't get in my formal education, I learned by reading. Books are amazing—either the real ones or the electronic ones—but I prefer holding all the knowledge of the real ones in my hands and learning anything from them that I'm curious about. Also, Godfrey, my health is good, and emotionally I'm fine. It's a wonderful thing when you're free enough to be spontaneous, and I am, partly because my lovely daughter here is the only one I hold myself accountable to, whether she likes it or not."

"I have to say," Marvel chimed in, "I love that Dad includes me in some decisions and occasionally even asks my opinion. I don't think there's an answer to your question though, Godfrey. It's just how Dad is! He's a giving guy. He won't tell you about the good he's done, but he's helped many people and solved multiple problems. He manages to somehow stay the unknown benefactor in all cases too, and I guess that's the biggest reason I'm so proud of him. He loves New Orleans and would do anything for the city and its people. He's a Saints fan to the core, and during football season, he buys Saints tickets just to give them away to people who need to escape problems and have a good time. And during Mardi Gras, I'm constantly being thanked by Mardi Gras krewes for his contributions so citizens can enjoy the fun of riding on floats."

"Yes, but they only know you're my daughter because you carry the name," Tarlton interrupted. "Marriage could change that, you know."

"Something else about my dad," Marvel continued with a laugh, "he always gets special pleasure out of urging me to find the right guy, all the while knowing that he and I are both completely content being unattached."

"There's certainly nothin' wrong with bein' unattached. Some rather it that way," Godfrey laughed. "Now. tell me if it's none of my business, but can I ask what happened to Marvel's mother?"

"It's quite all right," Tarlton answered. "Marvel's mother and I have been divorced a long time. She moved away soon after and later remarried. I know that because that notification eliminated my alimony payments. She and I split when Marvel was little and I was granted custody, so Marvel and I were our own little team, which gave me time to spoil her. Over the years Marvel has had many friends but not much family—for I have no siblings. My parents have both died, my mom the most recent, in Katrina. She lived in the Lakeview section of New Orleans, where I grew up, in the house I was raised."

"Oh my gosh, then she lost everything!"

"Oh yes, and she had much to lose. She was surrounded by lifelong friends there. Her family was fairly wealthy, so she'd been a debutante and a maid in several Mardi Gras krewes and even had an entire room full of all that memorabilia."

"But more importantly," Marvel interjected, "some of her closest friends died in flooded nursing homes. She lost one especially close friend who drowned in her home a block away from Mother's. The friend was overweight, and we figured her weight must have made it too difficult to maneuver above the flood waters. She loved beignets and fried seafood, but always blamed her weight on her medication. Everyone knew better."

"Yes," Tarlton continued, "Mother would worry about her and warn her, but at the same time, she also understood and shared that love for great food. Mother evacuated with Marvel and I before Katrina and lived in my house while I had her house gutted and redone. But she was never the same person again. Marvel even moved back in to try to bring her some additional happiness, but she was completely heartbroken. She tried valiantly to stay in good spirits, but was apparently too distressed to overcome it. She kept envisioning her good friend in that terrible situation and had recurring dreams about it. Had Dad been alive, he might have made things more hopeful for her, but she didn't even live long enough to see her house completed."

"Yes, Godfrey" Marvel added. "We watched that vibrant, energetic, elegant woman, wither into a tired, despondent someone we no longer knew, for she had no interest in even the most normal things."

"But let's not keep this so sad," Tarlton inserted, "for we know she's in heaven now, reunited with Dad and her friends."

"It was so awful for so many though," Godfrey added somberly, "and much worse for the older people. I can relate to how it must have been to lose everything when you know you no longer have the strength or endurance to start over." He then quickly wiped his wet cheeks with his rugged hands, sipped his wine and tried to say cheerfully, "Now, Tarlton, tell me what you were trained for in college. You know, what field were you in? And, by the way, are you in all those Mardi Gras krewes too?"

"No Mardi Gras krewes for me, Godfrey, although I was forced to be a page in many as a kid before I knew better. Hey, come to think of it, the pictures of me at the Mardi Gras balls are the only things I'm glad were lost in Katrina. And, to answer your question, my degree was from LSU in Business, and I became an investment broker, among other things. Now,

I was never a brain—always made average grades—never excelled, but as far back as I can remember, I've loved problem-solving. As the years went by, I seemed to want to take on one tough problem after another."

"Dad's really very versatile too, even knows music and taught me some," Marvel said, "although I don't measure up to what he can do with a piano or guitar. He's always saying everyone should have music in their lives."

"I agree, though I don't have that kinda talent myself," Godfrey laughed.

"You probably do," Tarlton countered, "but haven't had a chance to develop it."

"Yeah? Well, it's too late now. Anyway, I've always been a fixer-upper kinda guy. You know, I like to build things and draw plans to build 'em. I seem to go from one project to another. So now, tell me, what happens now with your Riverside project?"

"Well it's more than ready to go, with contractors, workers, and everything needed all lined up. Riverside's the perfect location and my real estate agent and parish officials are trying to come up with the appropriate property for it. I've learned that, once I've put my cards on the table and done all I can do, it's best to sit tight and wait, so that's what I'm trying to do right now." After emptying his wine glass and checking his watch, Tarlton rose and apologized for staying so late.

As they all stood, Godfrey grabbed Tarlton's hand, shook it vigorously, and said, "Tarlton Daunois, I have to say, I'm proud to know you. I admire what you've done with your life. You seem like an up-front guy and I wish you luck in findin' your location."

"Thank you, Godfrey. It's been a pleasure getting to know you."

"Please do come by anytime, and you too, Marvel. We'll see about the puppy for you, but come by even if that doesn't work out. I'm sure Flex'd like seein' y'all often."

After they left, Godfrey went to bed planning to call Ilana at the hospital gift shop the next day. Of course, because of Flex's excitement at breakfast about Marvel possibly getting a puppy, Godfrey had to promise him he'd call her as soon as Flex left for school.

"Hi, lil lady!" was Godfrey's greeting when Ilana answered his call.

"Well, hey, Godfrey! How're things?" Ilana answered as she rang up a purchase.

"Things are great. Met some new people last night and now I have a question. By now aren't you at your wit's end with puttin' up with two dogs at your place and aren't you anxious to get rid of the last little flower, Chrysanthemum?"

"No, not so much. The last little flower—namely Jasmine—wants to play a little too much for Blossom though. Why? You're not by any chance missing Blossom?"

"Oh no, no! But Flex has found someone he'd like that little flower to go to, if you're at all interested in letting her go."

"Gee, this is a surprise. I've gotten so used to both of them, I'd have to think about it. Tell me about who it is he'd like to have Jasmine. Is it the new person you've met?"

"Yeah, her name's Marvel and she's thinkin' it over too—I mean whether she'd even want a dog. You'd like her though—very nice girl."

"Okay. I've got another customer now, Godfrey, so I'll get back to you about it."

Ilana had only considered life without Jasmine once, about a month earlier when Addison was at the townhouse and mentioned that he and his high school girlfriend, Lark, had reconnected. During that discussion, and while playing with Jasmine, he mentioned that if it got serious enough to warrant marriage plans and a house purchase, they might be interested in having Jasmine. Not long after that, a disappointed Addison called to report that Lark wasn't a dog lover.

Lark lost Ilana's favor originally when Addison dated her previously and they split when Lark confessed she'd been secretly seeing Frank, an older guy from Houma. Addison was crushed, so obviously Ilana hated seeing him apparently willing to give her the opportunity to hurt him again. Despite a slight hostility she felt toward Lark, as any mother would understand, Ilana, *nevertheless,* remained congenial toward her for his sake. She reflected on them after Godfrey's call and then again while driving home.

She was still entertaining those thoughts as she entered the townhouse to find Jasmine jumping up at Blossom to grab her ears as Blossom growled softly. For the first time, Ilana wondered if Blossom would be happier not having to dodge the puppy's playful tugs and constant beckons for attention. Would she herself also enjoy the change?

On a daily basis, Ilana dealt with traumatic emotional situations at the hospital and then faced more trepidation at the animal shelter. It was important that her off hours be stress-free, and she had to admit that Jasmine's exuberance often tried her patience. Although the bad times at work had been rarer than usual lately, giving her more relaxed free time, and Godfrey happened to call at a good time, she knew she should focus on the most trying of her after-hours, those when Jasmine's antics really annoyed her.

After focusing on the two dogs for a day and night, Ilana made her decision. She called Godfrey the next morning to say, "You can bring Marvel over to see Jasmine anytime. I'm now ready to enjoy life with one calm and settled older dog only."

****

Ilana and Godfrey planned the meeting between puppy and prospective owner for the following Friday night when Godfrey and Flex would bring Marvel over to Ilana's. Normally witnesses aren't necessary for a dog ownership transfer, but a substantial number of people showed up that night. No one doubted Marvel's instant love for Jasmine, so everyone knew their goodbyes to the little furry bundle were in order. Ilana's neighbors came to say they'd miss Jasmine in the courtyard; Ilana's friends, who'd also become attached, were there; Addison showed up with chew toys and a leash he wouldn't need; and Amelie brought the vet she'd been dating, in case Marvel had questions.

As happens in South Louisiana when people get together, a party soon develops. Ilana began popping popcorn, brought out cheese and crackers, prepared a pitcher of lemonade, and poured wine. All enjoyed getting to know each other better while sharing dog stories—and this was before Marvel, Godfrey, and Flex arrived. When they did, Marvel handled the pup's enthusiastic friskiness easily. Amidst Jasmine's face licks and everyone's cheers, as Flex had predicted, an immediate mutual attraction was apparent.

Only noticed by a few, there was an additional attraction that night—between Marvel and Addison. After everyone left but Amelie, her date, and Addison, Amelie snuggled up to Addison and asked, "So, big bro, when will you be seeing Marvel again?"

"Okay, Sis, I'm going over there tomorrow, as a matter of fact, because I noticed a strange noise in her car's engine when she drove up. The mechanics who usually fix it are going to an out-of-town festival, so I told her I'd see what I could do. Flex wants to come to help me work on it, and Marvel's offered to fix us lunch as payment."

"Oh, and what will Lark say when you tell her you're going over to Marvel's?"

"We never do anything on Saturdays anyway because Lark's usually shopping."

"You REALLY didn't answer my question, you know. I asked…"

Ilana giggled from the kitchen, "Now, Amelie, you know it'll give Addison more time to spend with Flex."

"Oh, right!" Amelie smirked playfully, "Sure! He'll have more time with Flex!"

CHAPTER ELEVEN

The holiday season brought South Louisiana its usual snow-free merriment as old friends again partied together and new acquaintances became closer. The New Year arrived with loud blasts of fireworks and horns and the quieter, more sedate resolutions.

Thanksgiving thru New Years celebrations were as wonderful as they could've been; *nevertheless,* not distraction enough for Tarlton's go-getter spirit. He could only think about getting his Riverside project up and running. He had commitments from contractors and their usual crews, plus a surplus roster of others wanting any available helper jobs. There was even a list he'd already compiled of prospective paid employees he might use: background checkers, case managers, schedule coordinators, etc. He had everything—his ducks all in a row—everything but the most important: a location. Then, in mid-January, the parish president called with what was, to Tarlton, the final blow: No Riverside properties were available, nor were there likely to be any in the near future.

That call eventually spurred Tartlon into thinking his strategy possibly needed a different direction. Maybe what were needed were IMPROBABLE measures—like abandoning the idea of acquiring available property, and attempting to purchase land not listed on the real estate market.

That new thought process compelled him to drive over to the Riverside courthouse and ask for assistance from the Assessor's office staff. They showed him the Tobin map, an aerial view of land along the Mississippi River listing property ownership from prior to the 1970s. The individually-owned stretches of land seemed so similar in that they were mostly narrow sections of property extending from the river to the railroad track. These long, areas had acre-sized depths divided into what were called arpents in years past. People built closer to the road and river then, kept their livestock in barns behind their homes, and used the deeper sections farther back for farmland. Because Tarlton's plan included a circular driveway at the building's entrance, most of the land lacked the necessary width.

There were only two that could possibly work, but of course, both had the very obvious problem—they weren't available for purchase. Undaunted, Tarlton proceeded to the Zoning Department for further information on the closest one. He was told the front road-side section of the property contained two small rental houses and the remaining back portion was leased for farming. The probability of finding someone home at either rental house in mid-morning wasn't likely, but Tarlton drove over there undeterred.

He disturbed a teenage boy who was diligently attempting to reattach a worn-out screen to the upper half of a leaning outer door. Tarlton brought some tools from his trunk to help the boy align the door, and together they stabilized it successfully. When Tarlton questioned him about their landlord, the adolescent said it seemed the land had many owners now, and none were local, so no one ever showed up to check on things.

"Son, what usually happens in these cases, is that the original owner dies and the next generation becomes owners, but settle somewhere else. That generation of owners dies and the land ends up being owned by third and fourth generation family who, over the years, have relocated farther away. Sometimes they aren't even aware they own it, if their parents neglected to mention it."

"Well, all I know is that my mom has paid the rent by mail since we've been here. I quit school to take care of keeping things working because whenever she's put notes with the checks asking for repairs to be done, no one's ever shown up or answered at all."

Here, right in front of Tarlton, was the perfect example of a situation that could use the services of the live-in building arrangement he had in mind. This boy and his mother could live in the home while she worked and he attended school and did odd jobs. Their incomes could help finance his future college tuition.

Since the boy wasn't able to provide a landlord's name or address, Tarlton thanked him, gave him $25 as he shook his hand, wished him luck, and said goodbye. He then made the necessary return trip to the courthouse for further assistance from the appropriate department that could supply a landlord's name. This did result in the name of a possible contact, and he planned to pursue that lead once he got home, all afternoon if necessary. For the time being though, Tarlton only wanted to focus on lunch.

He drove over to Godfrey's and found him busy in his garage, but ready to eat, so they walked over to the diner where Ed, always ready for a break, also joined them.

Ed and Godfrey used the opportunity to enlighten Tarlton on their plans for a birthday party for Flex there at the diner. "We just got to thinkin' that he might not've ever had a birthday party," Ed began. "Maybe he did when he lived with his grandmother, but he was probably too young to remember it."

"Yep, these two old brains were thinkin' along the same lines, and sometimes that's dangerous," Godfrey laughed. "Since Flex has a birthday comin' up, we figured why not? We asked Ilana to organize it, and she agreed. She'll be great at it."

"Well, that's wonderful guys! A super idea! He'll love it!"

"He's a good kid, and a hard worker too," Ed went on. "He's made a lot of friends, and you know what's amazing? His great sense of humor! I can't figure how that could develop from such a sad start, so I gotta say Godfrey must have somethin' to do with it."

"I don't know about that," Godfrey answered, "but he is a conscientious lil fella. Sometimes he gets his homework done before he even comes home. He'll sit by the river and do it. He just loves spendin' time over there. Oh, Ilana would like it to be a surprise party, and Flex would get a kick out of that, but I'm not sure we can pull it off."

"You know what Flex would love?" Tarlton interjected, "and it WOULD be a surprise. I might just be able to impose on an acquaintance of mine to arrange for a tugboat captain to show up here during the party; wouldn't that be a thrill for Flex?"

"That would be the best!" Godfrey beamed. "He's always talkin' about those guys he hears out there on the boats. Please do what you can. Oh, and we want Marvel to be at the party too. We're puttin' together an invite list as best we can, so you two better Ipod it into your Blackberries, or whatever you do to save the date."

"We surely will," Tarlton chuckled quietly, as they all began eating their meals. "We'll both be looking forward to it!"

Tarlton left the diner with thoughts of party plans and hopes of his bringing about the best possible surprise for Flex—an introduction to a tugboat captain. He decided his afternoon was going to include two important searches: one for the perfect available tugboat captain and the other for the correct Riverside property landlord. As it turned out, after countless phone calls and some internet leads, both searches proved successful.

"Yeah, sure, I'm always ready for a party," answered one potential 'surprise' captain. "I'm even a little familiar with Riverside because I've dated a girl from there. You can count on me; I'm putting the date on my calendar right now and I'll be there."

"Now, understand me," Tarlton explained, "I don't want an apprentice; I need a licensed tugboat captain who mans a boat along the Mississippi."

"Oh, yes sir, I'm your man. I'll show you my papers," he answered. So Tarlton told him the particulars and they set it up.

Tarlton had to wait for a call back from a phone message he left at the landowner's number, and late that night a Miss Volch called. She was adamant in not wanting to sell the property, but only because she wanted the regular rental income to continue. She did admit, however, that the responsibility it entailed was becoming increasingly more of a hassle.

"Well, could we get together to discuss what I'm willing to offer?" Tarlton asked.

"Sure, I guess it wouldn't hurt, but I'm not even in touch with my cousins that I'd need to consult about it."

"Is there no one left I could speak to from the previous generation then?"

"Yes, actually even farther back. My grandfather lives in the nursing home here in Riverside, but doesn't say much. I've been handling things for him too by myself."

"Then please give me your grandfather's name and I'll go see him. You can join us if you like. I can be there tomorrow morning."

"Oh, wow, you're not wanting to waste any time are you?" she answered.

"Not one minute. Can you make it there for 9:00?"

She agreed, and immediately after their phone conversation, she looked up contact information on her cousins because she knew her grandfather wouldn't understand whatever plan Tarlton would discuss. If it turned out to be an opportunity for her release from the responsibility of handling the property, she definitely wanted their back-up. It took her the rest of the day and into the night to reach them all, however—and with unexpected results. When she mentioned the prospective buyer's name, most of her extended family knew of him and claimed he could afford to pay a considerable amount, a figure Lark considered exorbitant. She was stunned to realize there were such money-grabbing tendencies in her family and was in total disagreement with them, but decided to keep her feelings to herself and see what developed in her meeting with Tarlton.

At the conclusion of Tarlton's conversation with Lark, he immediately realized there could be a lack of understanding between their generations, since she seemed so young. Figuring Marvel would be the perfect person who could ease any friction, he immediately called and asked her to join him.

"Oh, Dad, it's going to mean even less time for me to meet my deadlines, and I'm backed up already. But, only because I love you and want more than anything for your dream in Riverside to happen, am I consenting to do this."

After Tarlton thanked her profusely, they hung up with the plan that he'd pick her up at 8:00 so there'd be time to ride by the property in question before going to the home.

CHAPTER TWELVE

As they walked from the car to the nursing home entrance, Tarlton mentioned to Marvel he thought it entirely probable that some people living here in this facility might eventually become residents in his live-in arrangement. The automatic door opened as a woman in a wheelchair maneuvered herself through it without looking up. "And this type door," he continued, "for instance, is a necessity for accommodating wheelchairs and people on crutches. We'll have them at all entrances."

"I know, Dad, you've mentioned it...more than once, by the way. It's to make the building compliant with...what's the Act? Oh yes, the Americans with Disabilities Act."

When they entered, the lobby area was almost vacant except for an elderly man very slowly shuffling his way past the entrance desk and a woman sitting behind it in green scrubs and writing on a clipboard. Tarlton told the woman they were to meet a Miss Volch, the granddaughter of one of the residents. She smiled, welcomed them, said she hadn't come in yet, and pointed out a bench on which they could wait.

The old man turned slowly toward Tarlton and called out, "Lee, it's you. You finally came. I've been hoping. It's been a long time, my boy. But I kept waiting."

"No, no, he's not your son, Mr. B," the woman in green told him as she took his arm and directed him toward where he'd been headed. "He's waiting for someone else."

"Well, he might want to play me a game of checkers anyway. Do you think?"

"Why, sure I would," Tarlton jumped up to say. "Anytime, Sir."

"Annie, please bring the young man to the parlor? I'll set up the board."

"Now, Mr. B, she answered, "The checker board is in the rec. room. There's no parlor here. Remember?"

"Oh," and he beckoned to Tarlton, "Young man, ON TO THE REC. ROOM!"

"Can I join you in a little while, Sir, after we've seen a resident and his granddaughter?"

"Oh sure, I'll head there now. I move so slow, I might be there just about the time you're ready to play."

The front door opened and a tall blonde beauty rushed in and looked around. "Are you by any chance Tarlton Daunois?" she asked as she studied him and Marvel.

"Yes, I am and this is my daughter, Marvel. You must be Miss Volch."

"Yes, but you can call me Lark. Nice to meet you both. My grandfather's room is just down this first hall. Oh, and maybe I should see if he's presentable before you go in." She led them to his room and entered first, calling, "Pops? I've got visitors with me."

A white-haired gentleman slowly came out of the bathroom and said softly, "Hello." As they found chairs and Lark introduced them, Tarlton proceeded to explain, very slowly, his interest in the Volch family property and clarified his plans for it. To be absolutely certain all was understood, he expanded his explanation to provide answers to any possible questions he thought Mr. Volch might have. *Nevertheless*, the man seemed to understand completely. He smiled at Tarlton but asked nothing as Tarlton handed him his business card with the amount he was offering written on the back.

Mr. Volch had listened intently the entire time without uttering a word. As he took Tarlton's card, he grabbed Tarlton's hand and asked, "Could I live there?"

"Why sure," Tarlton assured him. "I'm ready to start construction on the building as soon as I have some property to put it on. If we can agree on a price, I'll put a lovely comfortable home on your land for you and many others to enjoy."

The man smiled up at Tarlton and said, "SOLD!" without ever looking at the card.

"Now, Pops, you haven't even seen the price," Lark interjected while grabbing both of his hands. "Let's talk some about it and then we'll call Mr. Daunois. Okay?"

"Okay, darlin', but I really like what he wants to do," the man answered smiling.

"I can tell you do, Pops. That's the most you've spoken in a very long time."

They laughed as Tarlton said he'd expect to hear from them when they'd decided. He and Marvel said their goodbyes and left to head for the rec. room where they saw Mr. B waiting by a window and anxiously watching the arched door they walked through.

"Come on over here, Lee, and let me try to beat you like I used to," Mr. B called.

"Well, you might win, Mr. B, but I'm Tarlton, not Lee, and I'll do my best."

"Oh, yes. I don't know when I'll see Lee. You know, I taught him to play checkers when he was just a little fella."

"Well, Sir, I'm sure you taught him many valuable things he'll practice all his life."

"Yes." And Mr. B looked away as if attached to a lingering memory and caught by its permanent hooks. Finally he said, "Gosh, I sure hope so."

The checker game commenced slowly with Mr. B spending an endless amount of time seriously contemplating each move. The other residents tried to watch over some others in wheelchairs while Marvel spent the time compassionately watching the residents. She tried so hard, for her father's sake, to avoid thinking of the many things waiting on her desk back at the office. Not nearly soon enough for Marvel, the game finally ended with Mr. B winning easily and all applauding as Tarlton and Marvel left the rec. room and headed for the car.

"Dad, I've really got to get back to work. I didn't expect to be gone this long. That game lasted an eternity!"

"Oh, but Sweetie, I thought I could at least buy you lunch. We should celebrate."

"Dad, I probably won't have time to eat at all. I really have to finish up some things today before deadline. How about tomorrow, maybe even for breakfast?"

"Well, I'd love to go tell Godfrey the news, and you've wanted to let him know how Jasmine's doing. It'll wait though. Can you be at the diner tomorrow?"

"Fine, Dad. You make the arrangements and let me know, but you've got to get me back to work now."

"Shucks! And I was deciding whether to go see the real estate agent or the parish president first with the potential good news," Tarlton said as they drove across the bridge. "But I probably shouldn't get ahead of things until I know for sure they'll sell."

"Oh Dad, I'd say it's a given. I don't even think you really need to wait for a definite confirmation. That's how sure they sounded to me. But I'm glad you're willing to cool it a little longer and will wait to spread the word while I'm getting work done."

Lark remained at the nursing home so she and her grandfather could discuss this new development at length. Actually the discussion consisted of her delightedly pointing out all the advantages of selling the property as he listened quietly. She considered the offering price quite fair, and it was obvious what her grandfather thought of it. To ask for anything near what her cousins wanted might cause them to completely miss out on this opportunity for her to be free of the responsibility of the land. It seemed that once her grandfather signed the Act of Sale and whatever other legal papers necessary, the property would be off her hands and, as a result, out of her thoughts forever.

Mr. Volch's mind hadn't been challenged to think about anything this complex in some time, and at this stage of his life, he didn't really want to think about much. He knew he immediately liked Tarlton and instinctively trusted him. As for the price, he knew nothing of inflation's impact on property values, so the amount offered actually seemed like a fortune to him. He smiled every time he thought of it. Before she left, Lark and her grandfather agreed that she should contact a real estate agent to handle the paperwork for the sale. Her assuring him that she knew someone who could help her find one made Mr. Volch's smile even broader.

The phone rang at Addison's apartment that night with a disillusioned Lark on the other end. "I don't know what to do, Addison, and I also need your help in finding a real estate agent. You deal with them sometime don't you?"

"Yes, sure," Addison answered as he questioned her about the reason for one while drying his hair from the shower he'd just gotten out of.

"You know how I've wanted to be out from under the burden of our family property? Well, I got my chance, and it came out of the blue. We've got a buyer and my grandfather really wants this guy to have the property. The problem is my relatives want me to ask what I think is way too much money for it. But, Addison, they're not the ones having to deal with the hassles. You know how I get so aggravated with it. Pops is ready to sign the papers as soon as I get them, but, on the other hand, it might be foolish to not make as much money as possible off the land. I mean, maybe my cousins are right. Maybe he can afford more, but I'm so afraid if we ask any more, it'll completely scare Mr. Daunois off."

"Wait, what? Did you say Daunois? I've got water in my ears."

"Yes. Daunois—Tarlton Daunois is who's interested in the property and he's offered what I think is a fair price, but... Don't tell me you know of him too, and think he can afford to pay more."

"Well, yes, I do know him. And I know he's looking for property that he's got great plans for. There's a real need for what he wants to do."

"I know. It sounds fabulous and my grandfather even wants to live there, but...." She paused a while and then said, "You know Tarlton Daunois? You mean you don't just know of him? You know him? How do you know him?"

"I met him through my Mom and Godfrey. His daughter's the one who got the last of Mom's pups. Remember? Jasmine, the one I mentioned I'd like to have? They're really nice people and they both have great cars."

"Oh really?" Lark's voice turned suspicious in a flash as she continued, "How nice are they? How well do you know them?"

"I know them enough to know they're good people."

"How well do you know the daughter?"

"I saw her some."

"Have you spent time with Marvel Daunois?"

"I've only seen her twice."

"Addison, have you dated Marvel Daunois?"

"I didn't take her out. No! Hey, I thought you said you needed a real estate agent. Hold on and I can look for the number of a guy I know could help you."

"Addison Hayes, how much have you seen Marvel Daunois?" she pressed. "When did you see her? Was it when she got the puppy?"

"Yes, I brought some things over to Mom's with some things for the puppy I wouldn't be using."

"And then what other time did you see her?"

"I went over and fixed her car. It was making a noise and she needed it for work Monday. Her usual mechanics weren't available, so I worked on it. It's a great car, even a good color—kind of an orange gold with..."

Lark's jealousy rendered her speechless at that point and Addison only heard the slam of the phone. Seething with rage, she ravaged her purse for Tarlton's card, turned on the computer and e-mailed him to say that the family wanted $10,000 more than the amount he had offered.

CHAPTER THIRTEEN

That night Marvel called her dad to relay that one of her deadlines was extended because the specifications had changed, which gave her time to meet the other deadline in plenty time before the day ended. "I just wanted you to know, in case you felt bad about keeping me away so long. Also, if you haven't already, please make the plans to see Flex and Godfrey. But you do realize it'll have to be early, before Flex goes to school...."

"Hold on, Sweetie. I thought of that, but I wasn't going to plan anything until I heard from you. I figured you'd let me know when you got home if you were still up for it. And I'm so glad I didn't cause you the problems you expected. Actually this could wait, but I'm so excited to spread the word. I'll call Godfrey and get back to you."

"I understand, Dad, and as it turns out, I've got a few hours coming to me that I could've used today had I known I would've needed them. So plan away!"

Since it was a weekday and they wanted to see Flex too, Tarlton and Marvel's early visit to Godfrey's started about 7:00. It also included breakfast, since Godfrey had tempted them with beignets. Flex was all ready for school and anxious to hear about Jasmine, so he had questions for Marvel as soon as she and Tarlton walked in.

"Oh Flex, she's my little princess. I'm really so happy to have her, and she seems to like her new place. I've got her a pretty little pink bed, although she tends to sleep all over my apartment. But that's okay. And, by the way, I'm calling her Jazz for short."

"Cool! I told ya you'd like her. Hey, I knew you'd like each other!"

"And, Flex, Ilana did a wonderful job training her. I was so fortunate to get her after all the bother about that was finished. I guess I owe her big time!"

They fixed their coffee and sat down to breakfast, with Godfrey at the stove keeping the beignets coming as fast as Flex could wolf them down.

"Godfrey, they're great—just like always," Flex mumbled with a mouth full of powdered sugar.

"I see you've learned to eat beignets in your tee shirt—before you get dressed," Tarlton laughed. "Powdered sugar seems to show way too easy on colors!"

"Right! And, used to be, I never even HAD breakfast until I got to school."

"About that," Godfrey turned to say, "it's about time for you to get goin'."

"I know, God, but I sure wish I could stay."

"Oh, you'll see Marvel and Tarlton again soon. Now, don't leave without brushin' your teeth—and not just the ones that show!"

Flex soon came back into the kitchen with Chicory at his heels, gave them all hugs, and bounded out the door. He hollered 'bye' as he got on his bike. Chicory followed until Flex crossed the road, then quickly ran back at the sound of Godfrey's whistle.

Godfrey turned to explain he was expecting Addison at any time, since they were going guitar shopping for Flex's birthday present. In what seemed like only an instant, and before Godfrey could continue, Addison drove up, came in, and greeted them all.

"Boy, I must've missed TOO MUCH traffic by leaving so early, because I had to ride around a while until I saw Flex's bike gone. I don't think he would've looked back from the levee and saw me drive up though." He poured himself a cup of coffee and turned back around to see Godfrey handing him a plate of beignets. "Oh, and there are still some beignets left? Wonderful! Thanks, Godfrey."

"I hear you all are going to buy Flex a guitar. What's the story on that?" Tarlton asked. "Has Flex been asking for one?"

"Not really. Flex never asks for anything," Godfrey explained. "Whenever Addison comes to town lately, he comes over. He always has his guitar with him and he started messin' around with Flex and givin' him pointers. Flex really got into it and loves it, so I guess you could say Addison's givin' him regular lessons. A guitar seems like the obvious birthday gift, but it'll be a surprise, so we have to get it while Flex's in school."

"I had to rearrange some things," Addison clarified, "but this turned out to be the best day to be away from the office, at least for this morning anyway."

Marvel watched Addison intently, thinking how much she'd enjoyed being with him the day he fixed her car and how comfortable he somehow made her feel. She assumed there was someone in his life since he hadn't called her, so she continued to date occasionally and pushed him from her mind. Now, as she looked into his soft brown eyes, she realized she might never get him out of her mind.

"Now I was busy cooking earlier," Godfrey said, interrupting Marvel's thoughts, "so just how is our little Periwinkle doing these days?"

As she laughed at his choice of puppy name and before she could answer him, Addison asked her, "And I'm wondering how your car's running."

"Oh, I'm thrilled to be able to drive a silent car again, Addison, thanks to your efforts. I even took little Jazz out for a ride the other night and she loved it. And Godfrey, that little mischief-maker is a joy. She gets into things, but I love her to pieces."

While she elaborated enthusiastically about the car and the puppy, Addison found himself thinking how well the name 'Marvel' fit her.

Tarlton suddenly realized he hadn't yet checked his messages since he'd left so early, so excused himself to go to the car and see if anything on his Blackberry needed his immediate attention. When he came back in later, Marvel noticed a stunned expression on his face that she'd never seen.

"My gosh, Dad, what's wrong?"

Tarlton sat down heavily while sighing, stared at no particular site, and made hand gestures for her to wait for him to catch his breath. She patiently stifled a mood that went from anxious, to worried, to very upset, when her dad finally explained, "They're asking $10,000 more. I can't believe it. They were so pleased with what I offered. I can't handle an additional $10,000 without cutting corners on the building. I figured my price in accordance with the current construction market. Anyway, it was a very generous offer. How can they ask for more when Mr. Volch seemed so happy with everything?"

"But, Dad, not only him," a startled Marvel interjected. "Lark seemed so thrilled to be rid of the burden of the property. I can't believe it either."

"I don't get it. She sent this last night, too, not long after... I never checked for messages last night because I was so excited, and this morning I left in a hurry."

Addison had looked up quizzically, listened, and immediately begun to wonder: Could Lark have called him last night, hung up in a rage, and then immediately contacted Tarlton? He was still somewhat confused about why her mood changed so quickly on the phone. All he knew right at this moment was that he needed to think, so he went out the kitchen door and headed toward the old porch.

Godfrey came back into the kitchen from the panty and asked a still shocked Tarlton, "Man, what's wrong? Did Marvel upset you? Those gals'll do that you know!"

"It wasn't me, Godfrey. He's just gotten a shocking message," she answered while looking around for Addison.

"Anything you want to talk about? Tarlton," Godfrey asked as he sat down.

"Oh, Godfrey, you might as well know. My dream was so close and it just vanished, within the last half hour, matter of fact, and I don't know why."

Tarlton told Godfrey what had transpired as Marvel went outside to look for Addison. When she came back in looking confused, she didn't even have to ask Godfrey where he thought Addison might be. He pointed in the direction of the porch on the old house and said, "Marvel, I can't figure why he'd leave a pretty girl like you here to go sit on an old beat up porch, but that's probably where he is. Flex and his friends have worn a path to it by now, so it's easy to get to."

When Addison heard someone approaching, he looked up and smiled when he saw Marvel.

"Something wrong, Addison?" she asked. "I'm a good listener."

"Yes, I know that about you, and I like that about you too. I just need to wrap my brain around something I don't completely understand."

"I see. Well, I'll leave you to it while I look around here a little."

In a short while, when Marvel hadn't had time to go far, Addison called out, "Marvel, its okay. I know what I have to do. Let's go back in." He jumped off the porch, walked toward her, automatically grabbed her hand like he'd done it every day, and they walked back toward the house.

Tarlton felt he had to talk about Lark's abrupt decision reversal or he'd burst, so he and Godfrey discussed it thoroughly. Both offered possible reasons for her change of heart. None were convincing and some were not even remotely probable.

Marvel and Addison walked in and quietly listened to the conversation. Addison knew Tarlton needed any and all pertinent information, so he swallowed hard and proceeded to enlighten them about Lark's previous night's call. He couldn't make complete sense of it himself; *nevertheless* he wanted to help Tarlton with anything he could contribute. It almost turned into a debate from this new perspective with all except Addison coming to a conclusion: Surely Lark would reconsider, once she cooled down and thought rationally about it.

"No, she won't change her mind," Addison stated emphatically. "Lark will hold onto that property even though her grandfather loves your plan and wants you to have it."

"But, from what I understand, the property is a burden she wanted off her hands anyway," Godfrey exclaimed.

"It's just so insane for her to hold a grudge because of what's obviously mere jealousy," Tarlton added.

"I know that, Tarlton," Addison answered, "but I also know Lark!"

CHAPTER FOURTEEN

Addison received a frantic call from his mother that afternoon as he was getting back to his office after the quick trip to Riverside. He hadn't gone to see her as he usually did because there were so many deadlined architectural projects needing his attention.

Ilana had the biggest heart of anyone he'd ever known and she carried that heart on her sleeve, so Addison and Amelie learned early to avoid panicking when their mother was upset. He knew she was crying, so he asked her very slowly, "Okay, Mom, what happened? Did a dog die at the shelter today?"

"No, no, Sweetheart. I'm at the hospital today. That kind old man, Lark's grandfather, was admitted here and it really doesn't look good for him. Seems he got overly agitated and had some sort of attack. He's in ICU and I'm here with Lark in the waiting room."

Addison immediately realized his mother was probably the only one there with her. Lark's stepdad rarely left the house because of Vietnam War injuries; she was estranged from her step-sisters; and her stepmother traveled almost constantly in her work. Addison's mind stayed focused on the words, 'overly agitated'.

"Addison, are you still there?"

"Yes, Mom, but I can't come. I can call one of Lark's girlfriends to go over there if she's by herself."

"Oh, yes. She's by herself alright, with no family or anyone else at all here, but I'll stay with her if no one shows up."

"Thanks, Mom; appreciate your doing that," and he hung up, remembering what a great guy Mr. Volch was. Addison was well aware of the obvious cause of his attack and figured Lark was as well. He knew how she'd be feeling right now, but decided against calling her. Since his mother was willing to handle things there and he knew he couldn't allow himself any distractions, he got right to the unavoidable workload facing him.

Ilana had promised Godfrey she'd come by after work to discuss Flex's birthday party plans, and Amelie was to meet her at the diner later. So, when a couple of young girls showed up at the hospital and immediately went to Lark, Ilana was relieved to leave. Those feelings soon turned to sadness though, for before she left, she got word that Mr. Volch had died without ever regaining consciousness. When Ilana again approached her, Lark's mood had become so remorseful, Ilana felt compelled to stay somewhat longer.

She immediately called Addison to report the news as soon as she got to her car and then proceeded to Godfrey's, arriving much later than intended.

****

That evening Tarlton got an urgent message to call an unfamiliar number. When he did, a friend of Lark's gave him the message that he could buy the property at the price he'd offered. Since Mr. Volch's passing, Lark decided to do as her grandfather wanted.

Tarlton offered his condolences and hung up with conflicting emotions. He reflected on the sadness of the old man's passing, yet knew Lark couldn't sell him the property now at his price. Lark's biological parents were deceased, and she had told him her dad had no living siblings. Mr. Volch was the only heir of the previous generation. Actually, the decision was up to her cousins now because they would surely overrule Lark and ask a higher price than Tarlton could pay. If Mr. Volch had put nothing in writing before he died, the sale couldn't happen.

****

Addison didn't find time to go to Riverside until the day of the funeral, and Amelie took the morning off from work to attend with him—as 'the good sister'. Lark was lovely, even in her grief, but her face contorted into uncontrollable sobs when she saw Addison coming toward her. Throughout the funeral and burial, Ilana and Amelie offered what comforting words they could contribute as Lark held steadfast to Addison's arm. She was riddled with guilt, convinced she'd caused her grandfather's death. In her foolish rant against Addison, she'd gone to the nursing home and told her grandfather she agreed with her cousins to ask a much higher price.

Now she couldn't get his last disappointed and disapproving look off her mind.

"Oh, Ad, if he would've had the strength, he might've smacked me. Oh, I wish he would have! Maybe he'd have knocked me straight." She wailed as she looked into the distance, "Oh, Pops, I'll agree to sell at Tarlton's price like you wanted. I will. I'm sorry."

Had any of Lark's cousins been at the funeral and witnessed how distraught she was, they might have been inclined to compromise, but as far as Addison could see, no cousins from that side of the family had attended. Although he opted to not discuss it with Lark, he knew no signature from Mr. Volch meant there'd be no sale.

Before they had to return to duties, Ilana, Amelie, and Addison went to Godfrey's for a short visit after the funeral. Mr. Volch's death had been the talk of the diner, so Godfrey knew all about it. He welcomed them in and immediately started pouring coffee, as they settled around the kitchen table. They couldn't help notice opened albums and scrapbooks on the den sofa and coffee table. He brushed off their questions of why he'd obviously been looking at them, chalking it off to his being lonesome for not seeing any of the three of them in too long.

"Come on, Godfrey," Addison countered, "I only missed one guitar lesson with Flex, and I know Mom's been talking to you about the party a lot lately."

"Well, maybe it's not really being lonesome. That's probably really not it. Maybe I've just got things on my mind," was his unusual somber answer.

"Now, Godfrey," Ilana persisted. "Is everything all right? Were you close to Mr. Volch at one time? Did his death get to you?"

"No, no. I only knew him years ago very casually. My wife knew more people. She could've told you all his relatives' names. I'm fine, really! I was just looking at old pictures and reminiscing I guess." After more questioning, he continued to reassure them there was nothing wrong with his health, his family, his house, or his truck.

They did finally notice him loosen up somewhat when he began to kid around while getting caught up on their latest news, and he was himself by the time they said their goodbyes. *Nevertheless,* they all sensed he had something milling around in that head of his. They'd come to know that when Godfrey had something on his mind, he was a man who'd contemplate it in solitary, being distracted by his thoughts sometimes for days. They all knew he wouldn't share those thoughts until absolutely ready to, and all three left with no doubts that there WAS something,

That night Tarlton got a phone call from Godfrey asking if they could talk soon about something very important. Without volunteering any information as to the reason, he invited Tarlton over the very next morning. Once Godfrey had sufficiently reassured him there were no health concerns or immediate house or truck maintenance problems, Tarlton knew it was futile to ask further questions. They agreed on 9:00 as a mutually convenient time to meet, and Tarlton promised to rearrange some things in order to be there promptly.

CHAPTER FIFTEEN

Tarlton awoke the next morning, still stumped about Godfrey's suspicious request for this morning's meeting. *Nevertheless,* he quelled his curiosity enough to remember something he'd been meaning to do for a while. He made an earlier than usual phone call for in the morning, but he knew the one answering was up and functioning a long time prior. The owner of a new little hat shop in the French Quarter lived right above his shop and amiably consented to Tarlton's request to open early that morning and sell him a khaki cap. This particular cap caught Tarlton's eye months ago, but he kept forgetting to go by and get it. This morning he'd finally be crossing the river to Riverside with a long-intended replacement for the old, torn, paint-spattered cap Godfrey always wore.

Godfrey had the coffee ready and was pouring a cup for each of them as Tarlton walked in carrying the cap in a bag to present to Godfrey later. He intended to avoid spending time on hat discussion when there were obviously more pressing matters.

After greetings were exchanged and both were seated, Godfrey asked, "I have to ask you something, Tarlton. Why is this Riverside home project so important to you? I mean you've come up with this whole building idea from scratch and now you're dealing with a maor property search. As far as I know, it's something that's never been done before and it's been a real battle all along. And now that you can't get the Volch property, what will you do?"

"Well, my quickest answer to your first question, Godfrey, about why it's so important to me is just that available talents and skills are being terribly wasted. About the loss of the Volch property, I do have a chance at a piece of land, but it's too narrow in front footage, so I'll have to completely revise the plan dimensions to make it work."

"But, Tarlton, if people took the time to think about it, everyone would realize talents and skills are being wasted. There are all kinds of problems that need fixin' that nobody's doing' anything about. For instance, teachers all over the country ought to be makin' more money than anyone else because what they do is more important, but no one's doin' anything about that. What makes you care enough to want to do something to make things better? You've come up against all these property hurdles. Why do you even want to bother?"

"Oh, but Godfrey, that's pretty much the bottom line. Believe it or not, I've given it serious thought at idle times in the past, and this is what I come up with." You see, I'm convinced my being alive and well today is for a purpose."

"Okay now, you're goin' to hafta explain that a little more clearly."

"Well, I was told I was a miracle baby. The story goes that my mother fell in love with a guy from Lafourche Parish. She left her wealthy home and family security and they eloped to his farm life there. Her family, of course being very much against it, claimed she jeopardized my birth by abandoning the city's better medical care in New Orleans for the hard farming life. I was born with serious problems and wasn't expected to survive, but somehow I did. My mother told me when I was older that she and my dad wanted more children, but she had many miscarriages."

"I see," Godfrey responded seriously. "I know there were many young families struggling with farm life in the South. Go on, please!"

"Of course my mother and father were happy and did alright, but never lived in comfort like she'd known when growing up. Anyway, who knows if they could've had more kids, even with better medical care? I can't help feeling that I was meant to survive in order to accomplish important things in my life."

"And how did you come to see a need for what you want to build?"

"When I watched Marvel go out on her own and independently insist on no monetary favors from me, I became more aware of the conflicts one faces in just trying to make it. I mean, good people want only to make a living in order to be comfortable, but they can't afford transportation to get to a job. Others have talents and could go far with training, but have no financial means to develop their skills and no available family to help. I could go on about different circumstances, but I'm mostly concerned about the danger of it all, caused by two things: The frustrated youth who resort to crime just to survive, and the elderly who become so lonely and despondent, they attempt suicide."

"Tarlton, I loved your idea when I first heard it, and hearin' your reasons makes me know for sure I want to be a part of it. It seems to me, land couldn't be put to better use. My parents, my brother and sister, and especially my wife—I know would all truly want your project on this land."

An astonished Tarlton emitted a shocked response that stumbled out as, "What? What are you saying? Godfrey, it sounds like you're wanting to sell me your land?"

"That's exactly what I'm wantin' it to sound like. I figure it'd work for what you've got in mind. Matter of fact, I wouldn't mind livin' in what you're plannin'. I'd like to be your first resident!" he proudly announced. "You know, I've been asked to sell this property for commercial use a few times, and I was offered a pretty penny for it too. I could've made a bundle, but I didn't like what they had in mind for it."

Tarlton's coffee was cold when he noticed it again after listening to Godfrey's shocking proposal. He sipped it clumsily and said, "Godfrey, that'd be great! I mean if you're sure about it. But, what about your daughters? What will they think?"

"They'll think I'm not old enough to stop living alone yet, and probably won't want this house taken down. When they realize how important it is to me and see the good it'll do, they'll be fine with it. If not, I can always get Ilana to talk to them; she's good at that sorta thing. Oh, one important thing though, Tarlton, I have a condition that goes along with the offer. I really like what I hear about the energy-efficient homes, the ones with the green material. I'd want to see a lot of those ideas go into your plan."

"Godfrey, you're going way overboard here on being a man after my heart! That's exactly what I intended! Oh, and you've made this house way too nice a place to tear down. I'd incorporate it into the plan, maybe to stay as a building to work out of during construction."

"Wonderful!" Godfrey answered. "Oh, this is exciting! It just gets better! I'm ready to get this whole thing rollin' so how do we actually go about it?"

"Well, since no changes are necessary, and if you're agreeable to what I offered for the Volch property, I can leave it in my lawyer's hands. I'll get him right on it."

"Hey, Tarlton, why don't you bunk here with Flex and me during the construction so you'll always be on site?"

"Great idea! I'd want to be here every day supervising and keeping things humming. I'll hardly be here though—just to shower, sleep, and grab a sandwich. Oh, this is fantastic! Wow, we should celebrate! Oh, by the way, I hadn't planned it this way, Godfrey, but I just happened to bring you a commemorative gift for our new venture."

Godfrey immediately adjusted the cap and wore it proudly as they toasted coffee cups to this new news that would finally enable a dream to come to fruition. Tarlton brought his plans in from the car, for they were always with him, and unrolled them onto the kitchen table. After they looked them over a bit, Tarlton called his lawyer and notified parish officials. Godfrey called Ed over from the diner and had Ilana come by after work.

Godfrey's daughters were thrilled with the news, once they understood the building's purpose—uniting the youth with the elderly to effectively use the skills of both. They knew it was something their mother would've, not only approved, but would've adamantly encouraged.

CHAPTER SIXTEEN

For weeks Ilana planned Flex's birthday party, efficiently making lists to insure she'd thought of everything. She'd already sent invitations to the known addresses and others were invited by phone or word of mouth. Her hope was that no one important to Flex was being inadvertently left out. Amazingly, everyone was keeping that it was a surprise hidden from him, so it seemed it might turn out that way after all.

Her regular volunteer work and party-plan preparations were completely filling Ilana's time, but soon she discovered an addition to her responsibilities. Right after hearing the news of the land sale, Ilana was asked to supply a suitable name for the place 'since she was so good at those things'. It seemed Tarlton had thought of everything in planning this dream of his—everything but a name!

Nevertheless, Ilana found herself not really minding these additional duties because both the party and the building project were important to her, simply because they involved such special people. She'd come to love Flex like another son because he was such an irresistible kid who appreciated every little thing. This birthday would almost be like his very first because he couldn't recall much about any others. Probably his last birthday came and went, again with no recognition, like all the others. That might have given him the push he needed to escape his past and ultimately become an important part of their present.

For her chance meeting with Godfrey, Ilana would be eternally grateful, partly because she realized how much he reminded her of her dad. Godfrey had her dad's diligence toward a task, persistence as it developed, and then a quiet pride upon its completion. As a child, Ilana watched her father build many desks, cabinets, chests, and armoires for others after his regular work hours were over. A plain man, yet one not easily influenced or intimidated, he was always Ilana's rock who would approve or disapprove with a look or expression only she would recognize. Since deceased, her dad remained her guardian, for she thought of him sitting on her shoulder. Much like both Godfrey and Tarlton, her dad worked hard all his life and quietly helped many, without drawing attention to himself. Whatever work ethic she had was instilled in her by him.

Tarlton, the man who had all the charitable traits she admired, was also the man with the intelligence and the means to see his insightful idea materialize. Despite the obstacles he'd faced, this man with a project that would benefit so many, was also making Godfrey a happier man by putting that project on his land.

From what Ilana'd been told, Godfrey's parents purchased their land for what would seem like a meager amount now. Wouldn't they be pleased to know what's about to happen to their investment—the base for a home some would otherwise never have. Young people with unstable home lives and financial problems, and older folks with knowledge and unused capabilities would live there together, in a cooperative alliance. All could develop their potentials while living in an atmosphere of shared cooperation.

The young would attend school and hold down after-hour jobs as the elders tended to household things—all while combining their talents and incomes to nurture each other in a comfortable home. Those with day jobs and small children could work full-time while their babies were safe and well cared for by other residents.

Ilana witnessed many struggling families in her volunteer jobs, so she knew well the benefits to this teamwork idea and the structure and safety it would provide for the adolescents. As she thought more on the request of naming this promising place, she began to consider it an honor. If she had the perfect name in time, it could be announced at Flex's party. If a sign with the name could be made in time, they could present it to Tarlton at the party!

****

Tarlton and Godfrey spent the following week salvaging whatever was usable from the old house and marking trees and plants they didn't want disturbed. By the end of the second week, the weary structure—old porch and all—had been torn down, making way for clearing the land and filling in the low spots. By the third week, marking stakes were put in and plumbers and electricians brought in.

It was happening fast, and was the talk of Riverside. People came by to ask about helping to build it and of moving into it. If Tarlton wasn't around, they were given his number to contact later and sent away with a wonderful impression of the future there.

When Tarlton originally told Marvel about his project, she assured him she'd be willing to resign from her job to help get it started. Though he didn't want her to completely abandon her job, in time he found he needed her to handle the paper work, which she came to enjoy immensely.

Since the plans had been drawn long ago, Addison figured his architectural skills wouldn't be needed, even though he was anxious to help. He was thrilled when Tarlton asked him to be a consultant as construction progressed and to help out with whatever interested him when it was completed.

Amelie enthusiastically offered her services if Tarlton agreed to raise chickens, cows, and goats on the land for eggs and milk to be used at the home. She also felt the property's size—very narrow yet miles deep—was perfect for training horses and teaching horseback riding. She knew it would be a worthy addition to the collection of skills being taught—if not for now, surely for in the future. Tarlton had so far only agreed to the chickens, cows, and goats.

Already, Ilana knew someone wanting to become a resident, a cosmetologist who had to beg rides from everyone to get to her New Orleans job. If she could live there, she'd cut all the residents hair, and possibly find a local cosmetology position until she could afford a vehicle. The mother and son from Lark's family property rent house definitely wanted to be residents, along with Mr. B and others from the nursing home. Skilled brick-layers, floor-tilers, and carpet layers, struggling to pay apartment rent were also extremely interested. They all had jobs, but couldn't find rooms they could afford.

Almost daily, Flex came home from school reminding Godfrey and Tarlton of his friends at the foster home's desires to handle lawn maintenance. Some of the girls offered their talents in jewelry-making and other crafts, and one of Flex's teachers wanted to live there and tutor and teach knitting.

Everyone involved ultimately started lists of interested people, and Marvel was efficiently keeping all information organized as the lists quickly lengthened.

Serious discussions were coming up between Godfrey and Ed about Ed's closing the diner and living at the place. He felt ready to take that important life-changing step and had already discussed it with his family. Godfrey, though definite about his own move, cautioned Ed about whether the time was right. It would mean Ed's leaving a business he'd handled for years, and Godfrey wanted him to be positive he'd have no future regrets. Godfrey and Ed were long-time close friends, even though they currently only saw each other occasionally when Godfrey went to the diner for meals. They cherished their shared memories of their wives being friends also when the four socialized together in their younger days.

Picturing how it would be—their living there—seemed to help them ensure each other it was the right move for Ed, so they'd spend time envisioning it. Ed would do most of the cooking and Godfrey would handle repairs and any woodworking. They'd both raise vegetables and fruit and preserve them, while teaching anyone interested how it's all done. In their spare time, they'd take residents fishing, thus keeping the freezer supplied with fresh fish for their group meals. Of course, this was with their mutual agreement that they'd be teasing each other as they'd laugh their way through it.

Ultimately, the decision was made that Ed would take the plunge and give up the diner. He offered it to his kids, and planned to sell it if none wanted it, for he was definitely ready to retire and let someone else handle its responsibilities.

CHAPTER SEVENTEEN

The black lettering on the yellow sign read 'SOUTHERN SHARE-WAY.' Not only had Tarlton approved the name Ilana had chosen, he considered it perfectly appropriate, since he hoped its success here in the South would generate a Western, Eastern, and Northern Share-Way.

"I know it's enormous," Ilana told Blossom as she leaned it against her den wall, "but maybe it only seems too big because it's inside." Blossom had barked at it the whole while she watched Ilana struggle to bring it in. "Anyway, it's too late now. And even if the size is wrong, I know the color's right," She recalled Marvel once mentioning her father's favorite color, thus rendering yellow the indisputable color choice.

Ilana made herself some tea, stirred in some honey, and took it to the sofa to rest a while with her cherished pet's head on her lap. She recalled the time and work involved in completing this enormous wooden masterpiece after she and Godfrey decided a sign was an absolute necessity. It was a joint effort between the two that they'd managed to keep secret from Tarlton, and then contrived to have its presentation to him be a surprise.

Godfrey, Ed, and Ed's sons moved the tools Godfrey needed for making the sign from Godfrey's garage to Ed's. After all agreed it should be the size of a transom over an old plantation door so as to be visible from the River Road, Ilana and Godfrey selected the perfect piece of cedar at a cabinet shop. Godfrey meticulously cut and sanded it to expertly curve its edges while Ilana experimented with various letter styles for a sketch Godfrey followed with his router. And Tarlton never noticed!

It was all to happen this evening: Flex's birthday party and the presentation of the sign. Flex knew about the sign, and Tarlton knew about the party, but neither knew of the other. An announcement of Share-Way's current status and the sign presentation were to be made only after the birthday celebration was complete. It seemed appropriate since the party was going to be at Ed's diner and it would include the revelation that Ed would soon retire and pass the diner onto his two sons, who would share ownership. Demolition and then enough construction had progressed on Tarlton's building so everyone knew what was happening on Godfrey's land. However, few knew that Ed and Godfrey would be its first residents, so that would be an additional announcement.

Ilana hoped Tarlton would think the sign perfect, for she thought it was—despite her concern about its size—and she couldn't believe how anxious she was to see his reaction. Somehow the sign seemed to her the most important of all the things she prepared for Flex's party—and it had nothing to do with Flex's birthday.

The plan was for Godfrey to take Flex to an IMAX movie that afternoon, with Flex believing it was his birthday gift, and they'd stop for snowballs on the way home. Flex had lived with Godfrey long enough to know how Godfrey diligently watched his money and limited his purchases, so Godfrey's actual birthday gift would be a definite shock to Flex. *Nevertheless,* Godfrey would readily admit he only wanted the best for Flex and would do whatever made him happy. He knew how much having his own guitar would mean to Flex, so he bought him the best guitar of those Addison recommended, a Gibson--Les Paul, possibly the most exquisite instrument Godfrey had ever seen.

This being Saturday, and Flex's actual birthday not until Monday just about guaranteed he'd be surprised. Godfrey started cooking a gumbo that morning for the party and had made a huge bowl of potato salad the day before. Ed's sons were to prepare various salads and sandwiches, and Ed had promised his special chili. Once Godfrey and Flex left for the movie, the party would be in the hands of Ilana, Ed and Ed's two sons. Music was to be the old standby—a jukebox that now also played CDs, thanks to one of Ed's electronically-inclined friends. Ed wanted to keep the diner open for Saturday's lunch crowd as long as possible, so all the guests were asked to be at the diner by four o'clock to help decorate and set things up.

Ilana was first to arrive with decorations and requests for help in bringing into the diner her huge beautifully-wrapped package. Amelie and her boyfriend followed with a colorfully-decorated birthday cake they very carefully unloaded from his hatchback. Marvel and Addison showed up with jugs of ready-made frozen punch and immediately started making batches of daiquiris. Flex's foster home friends were soon tumbling out of the same van Flex had feared not that long ago. As other guests arrived and music played, everyone introduced themselves and proceeded to decorate and rearrange chairs and tables.

Tarlton brought Flex's surprise guests, a tugboat pilot named Frank and Frank's mentor, a riverboat captain everyone called Dock. When Frank agreed to attend the party so Flex could meet him, Frank mentioned it to the captain, who was so touched by Flex's story, he volunteered to come along as an additional surprise. As it turned out, Lark was Frank's date. Frank and Lark dated earlier but had lost contact. Since the party was to be in Riverside and Lark lived there, Frank took a chance she'd go with him. Lark agreed, and was looking forward to seeing Addison, Ilana, and Marvel again.

Opposite the wall of the jukebox were two tables, one held the cake and the other was soon overloaded with gifts. In the process of getting everything prepared and ready, the new acquaintances got to know each other better as they worked, so by six o'clock, it was a party! A few lookouts were watching at the windows for Godfrey's car to drive up at any time, and all waited anxiously to surprise, and possibly overwhelm, Flex.

Before long, as expected, Godfrey's truck pulled up to the diner and Flex bounded out in a rush, with intentions of telling Ed all about the movie. As he opened the door, a united 'SURPRISE!' bombarded him from all directions.

"Oh wow...whew...what...what's goin' on?" He hollered, as he stood stunned amid flashing cameras.

"It's your surprise birthday party, and I guess we might have shocked you," Godfrey said as Ilana ran to Flex and hugged him with all her might.

Seeing how stunned Flex was, Addison quickly went to him and asked, "Man, could this be your first experience with a party, especially one you didn't know about?"

"Woosh! You got that right! Gee, Ad, I can't believe this!"

"All your friends are here with gifts," Addison elaborated as he hugged him.

"And we've got a cake for you to blow out the candles," Ilana added with her tearful hug.

Everyone else came to him, one by one—some in tears—but all with open arms.

Godfrey looked for Tarlton as he said, "We all love ya, Flex, and

Tarlton has found two special guys we know you'll really want to meet, if I can find 'em."

"Say no more, Godfrey. Dock and Frank are right behind you!" Tarlton said as Godfrey spun around. We're anxious for you to meet these two guys, Flex," Tarlton continued, and introduced Dock, a riverboat captain, and Frank, a tugboat pilot."

"Oh wow! No! Really? Oh gosh! I can't believe it! I sit on the levee a lot and can hear you guys plannin' your day's schedule out there. Oh, this is the best! I listen to you all the time. I hope you can stay a while and don't have to get out there again soon."

"Hi, Flex," they both said as they shook his hand. "Don't worry," Dock added. "We'll get to talk. We'll stay as late as you'd like us to."

"And don't spell his name 'Doc'—D O C," Frank said, "because it's D O C K."

"That's pretty cool—because he's by the dock!" Flex answered. "I'm so excited you're here! But if I think about it, I'm really excited EVERYONE's HERE!"

Flex wanted to know from everyone how the party happened without his knowing about it, so all involved offered him their input when they could talk to him. At one point during the night he took his friends over to Godfrey's to see his room, where he proudly showed off Chicory and all his things. Dock and Frank spent some time telling him about the workings of river traffic, gave him their cell numbers, and agreed to stay in touch. What a special time it was for Flex! He probably ate more cake than anyone else, and no one saw him without a smile the entire night.

When gift opening was finished, Flex, awkwardly yet sincerely, thanked everyone for being there, for all the gifts, and mostly for being his friend. This instigated yells and whistles. When the cheering subsided somewhat, he added that he wished as much happiness for all his foster home friends, at which time the cheers re-erupted.

As everyone looked in one direction, that being toward Flex amid gift wrappings, Godfrey took the opportunity to gather Ed and Tarlton beside him. Ed and Godfrey then announced Ed's retirement and Tarlton explained the construction and the home's purpose for any who didn't yet know. Tarlton then said he had further important news: "These two guys, Ed and Godfrey will be Share-Way's first residents!"

The large package was then presented to Tarlton as all clapped and Tarlton asked uncomfortably, "What's this? Did Flex forget one?"

"It's for you, Tarlton, from Ilana and I," Godfrey called out over the rumble.

"I don't understand. Why would you be giving me a gift?" With emphatic urging, Tarlton carefully undid the bow and slowly removed the paper, as everyone tried to hurry him along. When it was finally unwrapped enough for him to spy the lettering on the huge piece, his mouth flung open as he exclaimed, "Oh, no! Wow! I never knew..."

"We thought you'd need one, so Ilana and I got busy on it," Godfrey explained.

"What? You mean you made this? No, you didn't. It's wonderful! Well, I mean, it's better than wonderful. Ilana, you too? You did this?"

"Yes, Godfrey made it and I painted it. I'm glad you like it!"

"Y'all have to see this," Tarlton gasped while proudly holding it in front of him.

Flex hollered out, "Hey, Tarlton, that sign was the only thing I knew about. I think you might be even more surprised than I was!"

"I believe I just might be, lil guy. These two people are unbelievable!"

"Man, I know all about that," Flex answered, "but in case you haven't noticed, Ilana's pretty too."

"Oh I noticed," Tarlton answered as he set the sign down on a table, thanked Godfrey, then walked toward Ilana.

Second-line music began playing. Marvel led everyone around the diner in doing the traditional New Orleans celebratory dance.

Before Ilana could reach the dance floor, Tarlton grabbed her hand and said, "I'm thrilled you did this for me," then, while clutching it tighter, "You're something else!"

"Oh, Tarlton, I think so much of your project and that you've even wanted to continue pursuing it after the obstacles you've faced. And Godfrey feels the same."

"Do you really like my project? I mean you've been supportive and all, but....you're doing all that volunteer work. Godfrey's got way more time than you."

"Oh, but that doesn't cost me anything, like what you're doing does. I love what your project will accomplish and think the world of you for wanting to do it...I mean..." And right away, she worried she'd said too much.

"Really, you think the world of me? I might have to let that sink in a little."

"Well, yes, Tarlton, you're a great guy!"

"Oh, now don't ruin it. Don't put me up high then right away knock me down."

"Well, I like what you stand for, Tarlton, and what you've done in the past, and I think you've probably got the biggest heart ever....and"

"Oh, if there's more, I'd love to hear it, but in someplace quieter. We're around way too much noise tonight. How about I take you somewhere really extravagant, sort of in appreciation for your efforts on the sign?"

Godfrey overheard this, and before anything else could be said, he interrupted with, "Well, nobody asked me, but that's even a better idea than your project, Tarlton!"

In response to Tarlton's questioning look, Ilana answered smiling, "I'd love to."

It was a wondrous night of memory-filled moments for not only Flex, although he was quite overwhelmed—especially by the guitar. It became a party not to be soon forgotten, and always especially remembered by Flex.

CHAPTER EIGHTEEN

"Hey, God, you know what?" Flex asked one Saturday morning while eating his pancakes. "A long time ago, tugboats toted barges—1870 I think it was, and they're really towboats, even though now they push instead of pull barges."

"You don't say?" Godfrey answered, while reading the morning paper and finishing his coffee.

"Yeah, and now they've got 10,000 horsepower engines; they use screw propellers and diesel engines now too."

"Uh huh. That's good!"

"And did you know that the captain's in charge of the boat, but the on-board pilot is in charge of the engine room, and you know what else he does? He figures out where to move the boat along the river."

"Oh really?"

"And years ago they didn't have buoys to signal about dangers in the river, so river pilots were really keel boat captains then because they knew all about any bad stuff in the river." After pausing and getting no response from Godfrey, Flex continued, "They had to be really smart too to know all that! Frank's grandfather was a keel boat captain and his father was a riverboat pilot, so they were really smart. Don't you think?"

"Sure," Godfrey answered as he reluctantly lowered his paper to finally look directly at Flex, realizing there was sure to be more information forthcoming. Flex couldn't control his enthusiasm since Frank, and Dock had just spent most of this clear southern morning walking along the levee with him. It was Flex's new friends' first visit since meeting them at his party and he'd waited impatiently for their arrival, even refusing to go off and play with friends in case he'd miss them. Godfrey would've loved some quiet time this morning while resting after finishing some yard work. *Nevertheless,* knowing he should be an audience for all this new knowledge Flex was determined to share, he feigned interest and commented, "Sounds like you learned a lot from those guys this morning."

"Oh, yeah, and they said they have even more to tell me. They've got pictures of places upriver they've been. They'll bring 'em over next time. You gotta see 'em too!"

"I'm glad they'll find time to come over again and I'd like to see the pictures. Now, kiddo, I know you're really excited about that, but since you're not workin' or off playin', maybe I should use this time to tell you somethin' I've been thinkin' about. It's about your job at the diner. I mean it's been good for you to have it and all. You learned about managin' your money and been able to save a little for college, but it really doesn't have to continue. The thing is, I'll need your help with whatever I can do to lend a hand to Tarlton now that Share-Way construction has started. There'll be carpentry work and a vegetable garden to plan out, and, you know, whatever else he'll need help with."

"But who's gonna buss tables at the diner? Ed says I do an exceptional job!"

"Oh, I know you do, but I'll need your help. I like havin' you as my assistant. They'll find someone. You could even recommend some of your friends for the job."

"Good idea! I'd rather help you, anyway. I do good work with you too. Right?"

Before Godfrey could answer, Tarlton called from outside the screen door, "Hey guys! Can I take you to lunch at the diner?" Godfrey waved him in as he continued, "I'm here to talk about taking you up on your offer, Godfrey, of bunking here, if it's still okay, while construction happens."

"Well, sure it's still okay—would love to have ya. Get your stuff and get moved in here whenever you like. Matter of fact, Tarlton, we were just talkin' about our helpin' you out however we can. Flex is goin' to stop workin' at the diner so he can be available."

"Yeah, put me to work," Flex added. "Hey, Tarlton, did you know Frank and Dock get paid a lot because they have to be smart about what's happenin' on the river?"

"Yes, I kinda did know that actually," Tarlton answered. "It's important that they know how deep all sections of the river banks are and be up-to-date on any disappearing landmarks and changes in the current. The

Pilots Association lets them know of any dredging and anything else that might affect the river."

"You know what else, Tarlton? Way back, I think they said in 1929, the pilot commanded the ship. The captain took care of the business and the passengers, so he only helped command the ship in emergencies."

"Really? Sounds like Frank and Dock have been here to answer your questions."

"And I've got more questions, so they're comin' back with pictures. But, now that I think about it, Dock'll be comin' back. I might not see Frank much because they said he spends all his time with Lark now."

"You know, little buddy," Tarlton answered, not at all apologetically, "I know about that because I seem to be spending a lot of time with Ilana lately. I find I want to be with her every minute. Frank'll be back, but he might bring Lark with him next time."

"Yeah, that's what'll happen," Godfrey added. "After all, we see Addison once a week for your guitar lesson and you notice how Marvel's always with him now?"

"That's right. So that means now I'll only see Ilana with you, Tarlton. Right?"

"Well, I surely hope she'll be with me more, especially now that I'll be staying with you guys on this side of the river. She wants to help with Share-Way, and she could help a lot, but it'll mean the hospital and animal shelter will have to manage without her. Oh, that reminds me, Godfrey, I'm thinking of having that little piece of yellow cloth framed, the one that drew Ilana's attention here in the first place. You don't care do you? After all, it was on your house, but it's special to me because I might not have met her, or any of you, if it hadn't been for that."

A surprised Godfrey exclaimed, "Tarlton, I didn't know you saved that scrap when they tore down the place. Now that you mention it, it is kinda special—to me too—because I wouldn't have met her or you without it. Aren't you somethin' to even think of savin' it! I'm so glad you're goin' to do somethin' like that."

"Well, it'll be more than just a framed scrap of material. Addison helped me compose a poem from some things I wrote down about my feelings toward her, and it'll go in the frame too. He's not only a great guitar player. He's good at coming up with song lyrics for the guitar, so I knew he could help me write a poem. I'm not sure when I'll give it to her though. I find myself looking for things that'd make her happy. I think about her all the time. She listens to all my crazy ideas and encourages me. She's very special."

"Oh, man!" Flex complained as he rolled his eyes, "Tarlton, -P-L-E-A-S-E-!"

"Little man, I promise you'll feel this way one day and you'll understand," Tarlton answered while playfully punching him, and then turned to Godfrey, "Can I bring some things over tomorrow to be ready bright and early Monday morning?"

"Sure! Anytime! You'll be in the front bedroom. You know, I might be gettin' a little scared and havin' some second thoughts about this new arrangement, now that I think about it."

"What? Should I not stay here after all?" an alarmed Tarlton asked.

"Why, Godfrey? What's wrong?" Flex asked, nearly choking on his orange juice.

"Well," Godfrey explained, "I'm thinkin' how it'll be. Flex'll be always rattlin' on about tugboats and riverboats, and you'll be talkin'mushy about Ilana all the time. I'm used to more quiet than that. How will I ever stand all that gabbin'?"

As Flex and Tarlton looked at each other, both stunned speechless, Godfrey blurted out a hearty laugh, "But I'll just hafta manage I guess! Just thinkin' about it makes me hungry though. What do you think, Flex? I thought I heard Tarlton say he was payin'. You want to go have lunch at the diner?"

"Whew," Flex sighed, "you scared me there. But, hey, what about Ilana? If I'll only see her with Tarlton now, can she come over and go with us too?"

Tarlton jumped up quickly to get his phone from in his pocket, "You know, I'm so glad you suggested that. I'll call and see if I can catch her right now."

"Gee, man, don't be anxious or anything!" Flex answered as Godfrey laughed and wrapped his arm around Flex's shoulders.

They left for the diner with Godfrey explaining, "You'll see someday, lil guy. It might start with a friendship, and then, even before you realize it, she's the only one you can think about. Before long, you become each other's support and strength that you soon come to depend on and eventually can't do without."

CHAPTER NINETEEN

Tarlton showed up at Godfrey's Sunday morning with what he'd need while living there at the construction site. He wanted his things organized in his room at Godfrey's rather than scattered at both houses. He felt extremely optimistic, yet cautious, for he planned to take a hands-on part in all aspects of Share-Way. Thus, he'd be completely responsible for any problems.

Marvel ultimately took a leave of absence from her marketing position instead of resigning. This was at her dad's insistence because he wanted her to keep the security of having that job if she wanted it again when Share-Way was up and running. She set up her office in the front of Godfrey's house in what had once been his living room, a room hardly used since he'd lived alone. Since a small den beside the kitchen was his real 'living' room, Marvel didn't feel her office was an imposition. She soon got into the routine of getting to the house early enough to have breakfast with her dad, Godfrey, and Flex before the day really got started at 8:00.

Marvel's Share-Way responsibilities entailed handling faxes and all e-mail and phone messages, plus keeping updated lists of potential workers and residents. Tarlton did all interviewing, from which he'd forward obtained information to Marvel. She'd follow up with a screening process she'd developed. She didn't thoroughly know Share-Way plans—only Tarlton did—but she knew enough to answer probable questions.

One morning, Tarlton found Marvel in her office more frazzled than she would've liked, for she was surrounded by buzzing phone lines and incoming faxes.

"Oh Dad, just a minute. Let me handle this call," she told him as she grabbed a pen and asked another line to hold. She then quickly took the call waiting as Tarlton felt compelled to answer another ringing line. She handed him a pen and paper, finished her call, while jotting something down, and then took another call and put another on hold. After Tarlton's phone conversation concluded, phones continued ringing, but Marvel seemed to handle them efficiently. Tarlton sat down to watch the action as she answered every phone while staying poised and helpful. When things went quiet suddenly for the first time since he'd walked in, they both looked at each other and laughed.

Somewhat embarrassed, Marvel said, "Well, I guess you had to find out that things get pretty hectic sometimes, but I knew they would, Dad, and was prepared for it. I just don't know how to put my hands on things I need quick enough yet. I've still got to get accustomed to the contents of my desk and files."

"But, Sweetie, should we get you some help?"

"No, no, please no! You just happened to come in at the worst time, Dad. I've learned now that calls come in about 9:00, of course the exact time you happened to pop in and see this chaos. But please don't think from that little show that you have to come in and help every morning at 9:00 now. Really, I've got this! And, believe it or not, I really do love the excitement of it all."

"Well, you handled that like a champ and I'm proud of you, as always. And now, I guess I'll be back again when I remember why I came in here in the first place, because right now, I have no idea."

Godfrey's duties were to build four wooden benches for Share-Way's entrance and several Purple Martin birdhouses that would be placed around the property. Tarlton's plan for both wood projects was two-fold, an obvious example of his thinking of everything. He figured future residents could learn how to build both of them and then sell them later. Since the benches couldn't be used until Share-Way was completed and the birdhouses were needed immediately, the birdhouses were Godfrey's first priority. Disease-causing mosquitoes are prevalent during South Louisiana summers, and those birdhouses would attract the birds that eat mosquitoes. The houses would be placed atop already ordered poles that would situate them high enough for Purple Martins to locate and easily get to.

In an effort to use materials in the 'green-building' spectrum, mold and termite-resistant wood, harvested from sustainable forests, had been ordered for the benches.

For placing in the shade of the huge oak tree—the one that held a tree swing years ago—benches made of permeable cement were planned.

Since the removal of the old house, the now clearly visible tree seemed even more splendid, standing in drapes of Spanish moss, as if waiting to veil someone in its shade.

"I plan to spend a lot of time under that old oak when all the work's done," Godfrey mentioned to Tarlton one morning. "It's a great feelin' to sit and enjoy finishin' a full day's work you can be proud of."

"And, from what I see you've already accomplished, you'll be worthy of a lot of time spent under that tree."

"Tarlton, I gotta admit though, I'm glad you decided to order prefab cabinets."

"Oh, I know, Godfrey. You're really good at building cabinetry and I know you wanted to build some, but I knew you couldn't handle that too. That's why I specified that they be installed on delivery. You would've wanted to put them up, and I didn't want you to try to do that either."

"Yep, I'm kinda glad you thought ahead about havin' them installed because every passin' year makes this old body surer that it just doesn't like liftin' much. Anyway, in my spare time, I'm kinda busy learnin' about the rain gardens we're gonna have here. I'm really curious to see the new-fangled way they're usin' cisterns to collect water for waterin' plants. Ya know, Ed and I are of the generation that actually USED cisterns, before people could get city water, so we both can't wait to see how it's done."

"I've heard about those old cisterns, Godfrey, and how people used the water for drinking and bathing. To think we drink water from bottles and you all drank water from a cistern that collected rain water along with the necessary bird droppings."

"Yep! And every Saturday night, all us kids bathed in the SAME water in a big galvanized tub. In winter we had to do it in front of the fireplace. But even in front of the fireplace, the water would cool. I had many very cold once-a-week baths. The water got colder and dirtier. That was another reason to try to get your chores done the fastest."

"So, makes you appreciate hot showers a whole lot. Right?"

"Yes indeed! And we'd pass around a hot water bottle to warm up our beds, and it was usually cold by the time it got to me. But, who knows," he asked with a laugh, "if it might've made us tougher? I gotta go meet Ed around back. We're gonna plan our vegetable crop. See ya later."

Godfrey found Ed checking out the sun's direction in relation to the markings for the kitchen. Nothing could actually be planted until the ground was safe from disturbance during construction. *Nevertheless,* Godfrey and Ed knew the importance of substantial planning and ground preparation before planting. They both wanted perfect placement for the vegetables so they'd get maximum sun and yet be close to the kitchen area. The best locations for the citrus trees and blueberries also needed to be decided.

To Ilana's dismay, Tarlton recruited her for decorating the lobby and choosing outside wall and trim colors. She didn't feel at all capable of making those very critical decisions but agreed only because of his and Amelie's persistent encouragement.

"I completely trust your judgment, Ilana," Tarlton kept telling her. "Don't let yourself get all wound up about it. I know you can handle it easily."

"Tarlton, it's wonderful that you have so much confidence in me, but I'm concerned because the initial impression is so important. I mean a person will see the outside of Share-Way first and then see its lobby. The appearance of those two things will give that person either a positive or negative feeling about Share-Way. Don't you see? The two things I'll be responsible for will be the very things that set the mood. Whatever happens after someone enters could be my fault. Oh, I can't believe you're entrusting me with such vital decisions."

He hugged her and immediately melted away all her defenses, "Now, I know you've handled things in the past that you would've rather avoided. How'd you do it?"

"In small steps is the only way I've been able to accomplish things. But you don't understand. I can't seem to find anything about this that's small. Everything seems so massive and important. Let me ask you again; give me some input—something, anything. At least tell me the colors you might like best."

"Well, if I must, I'll just say you don't have to be shy about your color choices."

"Don't be shy about colors? That has to mean no pastels, right?"

"Not really! I'd like you to choose because I know you'll make it perfect. It's just I guess my living in the Marigny makes me more accustomed to bold, dramatic colors."

"Bold, dramatic colors—bright colors—just about what I thought you meant! They're lovely, Tarlton, really, for there, but maybe not for River Road. Okay?"

"There you go! Right there! You've already started. You've got an idea what it should look like. Go with that. I knew you could handle it. Now

I've really got to get back to Godfrey's and get to my e-mail, so I'll leave you with those thoughts."

They'd had dinner at her place and cleaned the kitchen together while discussing it, so when he left, she immediately called Amelie—possibly for more convincing."

"Mom," Amelie encouraged, "You've got such a good eye for what's functional yet still looks nice. That's a special talent. Usually people can do either one or the other."

"Well, I've consented to do this, so now I guess I'm in, but I have to do it in small steps. Some small steps this'll take! I've never been involved in anything this big!"

"Mom, just remember how much you love decorating once you really get into it, and you know I'll help however I can."

"Thanks. I'm going to give it my all. I guess I'll first have to decide on the style of furniture and wall hangings that should go in the lobby; then I can select colors."

"Right, and once you pick the colors, you can order that environmentally-friendly carpeting Tarlton loves so much. I get a kick out of how he makes a big deal about that it's made of all recycled material. But Addison saw a sample and was very impressed."

"I know and I'm glad! I guess I'd order the carpet and have them hold it until we're ready for it—after the painting's done and before the furniture's delivered."

"I know you'll do a bang-up job, Mom. How about us going to pick up some paint color samples? I might even be able to help you decide on outside colors."

"That'd be great! Let's do it first chance you get. I just thought of something. I'd better have the hospital and shelter scale down my volunteer time. You know, Amelie, what I've been thinking I'm really grateful for? I mean in addition to the usual: That the individual Share-Way units will be unfurnished for residents to fix them as they like with their own things. Otherwise, Tarlton might have me decorating those too."

It quickly became well-known around Riverside that Share-Way's list of possible workers was much smaller than its list of potential residents. This was because of what Tarlton stipulated to those involved at one of their first meeting: "Because you'll probably be questioned about Share-way, you should know some things about those I'll be hiring. I've learned from previous projects who the trustworthy and dependable workers are, so, of course, I intend to hire those. Also, you already know how adamant

I am about using ecologically-friendly construction, whenever possible. To that end, all main workers hired will be those who are 'certified green professionals'. It's mandatory that they complete the Home Builders Association training course."

Considering it was the first time Tarlton ever attempted this type project, the first few weeks went smoothly. Everyone involved was amazed at his forethought, for they were constantly discovering things that proved he didn't miss anything in his planning. Everything he'd thought of beforehand ultimately made everyone's duties easier. As work progressed, each new aspect of construction seemed to guarantee everyone that Share-Way would be a completely successful endeavor for years far into the future.

Whenever possible, all materials used were "green" and ecologically friendly: insulated windows, programmable thermostats, spray foam insulation, energy-generating solar panels, and high-efficiency air conditioning with sealed ducts. All were used with the intention of minimizing the use of utilities.

During a break one afternoon, Godfrey, Ed, Tarlton, Marvel, Ilana, the workers, and Flex, who joined them after school with Chicory at his side, milled around relaxing. They were all enjoying their cold lemonade or iced tea while mentioning what they'd accomplished that day when Godfrey got the floor and thoughtfully said, "I hope you're all as proud of what we're getting' done here as I am. But, even when this is all complete, you know, there'll always be chores—house chores, yard chores, general maintenance of things. Hey, there'll always be weeds to pull. And, by the way, I look at weeding as kinda good for the soul. I like to think of it as gettin' rid of the bad to make room for the good." Everyone noticed Godfrey smile and wink at Flex at that point, everyone except Tarlton, because he was looking at Ilana.

Flex took Godfrey's cue, as they had planned for an opportune moment, and he and Godfrey chimed in together, "Tarlton, we're SO glad you didn't go COMPLETELY green."

"What?" Tarlton stammered, for that had gotten his attention. "But I have. I've...."

Before Tarlton could continue, Ed chimed in with them, "Nope! Share-Way's not COMPLETELY environmentally friendly green! Not entirely! Roof gardens would've made it COMPLETELY GREEN. And thank goodness it's too late to plan that now, because who'd ever want to climb up there and weed 'em?"

CHAPTER TWENTY

Flex hurriedly dressed for school as usual one morning, but with a much deeper concentration on what he'd wear—definitely not normal behavior for a pre-adolescent. He half-tied his sneakers and barreled into the kitchen with Chicory at his heels. Tarlton was sitting at the kitchen table in deep thought as he stirred his coffee. When he took a swallow, glanced upward, and noticed Flex's tee shirt, he almost choked.

"Aha, I thought this would get your attention," Flex laughed. "It was a birthday gift from one of the guys from the foster home. What do you think?"

"Whoa! It's a little sick, maybe creepy, but funny—"HAVE EDDY, WILL TRAVEL—ROUND AND ROUND, DOWN AND DOWN. Now since when do you have to wear a crazy shirt to get my attention? I live with you now and I'm here every morning and night. Is there a reason you especially need my attention today?"

"Well, yeah. I've got some friends—really, really talented ones—who could do you some good at Share-Way—I mean in painting. They're two guys from the foster home. One's always drawin' and scribblin' stuff. We call him Scrib and the other one is Doodles. We call their drawings Wonderworks. Doodles got in big trouble once for a big picture he drew on a bedroom wall. It was right before the people were goin' to paint the room, so he didn't think it would matter. Both of 'em just want to draw all the time."

"Having the talent to draw is fabulous, Flex, and only a few can do it well. Hey, they might even be able to help Ilana with decorating the lobby—maybe with a swamp or river scene mural. She's struggling a little with decision-making and might think it the perfect thing. Bring your friends over and let us see what they can do."

"Oh, thanks! They'll be so excited you want to see 'em. I promise, they're great!"

"We might even get them started in selling their 'Wonderworks.' And, you know what? Meeting with them will be a relief from what I've been dealing with."

"You've got problems Flex and I can help you with?" Godfrey asked as he came in from his morning look at the sky while drinking his last bit of coffee.

"They're just things I wasn't planning on doing, Godfrey. And actually you're doing plenty enough now. Did you know Amelie's pushing for us to raise goats for the milk? Though I'm thinking they'd probably do a good job of keeping the grass cut. Also she and her veterinarian boyfriend figure the land would be perfect, not only for teaching horseback riding, but also for breaking wild horses. That means I'd have to buy horses. Also Addison and some others are convinced swimming lessons are necessary, which means I'd have to put in a pool."

"Cool! Man, I can't wait for that!" Flex chimed in.

"Well, sure, little guy! Granted, they're all good ideas, but they're also things not figured into my current financial plan."

Godfrey looked over at Flex and said, "You better be gettin' your lil butt to school about now." And then to Tarlton, "Since you mentioned teachin', I've been meaning to tell you about somethin' my daughters would like to do. One of my girls would be willin' to do some computer training, and the other does the fancy writin'. I can't remember what you call it. But she's pretty good, and wouldn't mind teachin' it."

"You probably mean calligraphy, God!" Flex interjected on his way out. "My drawin' friends know about that. See y'all later!"

"That's great, Godfrey," Tarlton said, after they both waved goodbye to Flex. "We can use anyone who could teach a skill—like some retired widows who're wanting to give instructions on needlework—anything that can be taught without requiring a license. And maybe much more importantly, they won't cost me anything."

"Oh, and Ed knows a retired nurse who could give medical advice," Godfrey added. "I mean it would be only to let the residents know if they should see a doctor, but that would be helpful to older people and parents of young kids."

"Right, I know what you mean," Tarlton answered while adding to a list he was keeping on his Blackberry, an automatic reaction. "It would give them some guidance. I do appreciate everyone's thinking of ways to add to Share-Way's success. Ilana's also telling me people are coming to her with ideas. Maybe we should have everyone bring their people around all at one time for a discussion. We'll need to talk about what they can contribute and how we'll situate everyone so they won't be in each other's way. I'll need to mention that to Marvel and Ilana," and he added more to his Blackberry."

"Just a reminder, Tarlton: Ed's bringin' over muffallettas from the diner for lunch, and you don't want to miss that, so make some time."

"I'll surely try." Even though, just having finished breakfast, Tarlton's mouth watered as he thought of those round bunned sandwiches of ham, salami, provolone cheese, and olive salad, all covered in marinated olive oil.

"Oh, by the way, Godfrey, remember Mr. B? He can't wait to be a Share-Way resident, and I've kept my promise to play checkers with him at the nursing home a few times. The thing is, I don't know why his son, Lee, wants to see me first thing this morning. One way to find out, I guess, although I have no extra time today."

"I do remember Lee Bienvenu, Tarlton. He always was a nice kid— although I can't understand his not visitin' his dad more. But I guess we should both get busy. I've got to put a coat of primer on the birdhouse roofs. I'll see you later."

As Tarlton walked into the building amid the sawdust and hammer noise, an exuberant hefty man quickly approached him, arms outstretched, one hand holding snapshots.

"Good morning, Mr. Daunois. I'm Lee Bienvenu. You know my father from the nursing home. I'm so glad you've consented to see me. I can see how busy you must be here, but I've got something of grave importance to discuss with you because you might be one of the few who would help. You see these pictures?"

"Hello, Lee. Yes I see them, and I really like your dad."

"He surely thinks the world of you and says you can do anything. Actually, that might be why I'm here. You see, a lot of money was spent on the Louisiana coast, even before the Deepwater Horizon oil catastrophe. Money was wasted in the past, and then time was wasted with the oil clean-up. The coast must be fixed or the port of New Orleans, the oil refineries, along with the people, will have to be moved. These are pictures from the air. The pilots who've flown to and from the oil rigs see what's happening. This is what it was like in the 50s; this is what it's like now; and this is how it'll be in 50 years. And now of course the oil spill's made it worse. Hurricane impacts on New Orleans wouldn't be so bad if the barrier islands and swamps hadn't disappeared."

"Yes, Lee, I agree, but...."

"Mr. Daunois, the river needs to be opened up to the areas that used to flow through to it. Lafourche and Terrebonne Bayous are natural pipelines for river water to flow to the wetlands and that land can't rebuild without that river water."

"Right, so...."

"Before long, Baton Rouge and Mandeville will make up the coast, and everything south of those areas will no longer...."

"Wait, hold on," Tarlton broke in. "What in the world does all this have to do with me right now or with this building here? I've contributed to helping with the clean up of the oil spill in the Gulf, as frustrating as that's been, and that's all I can do now."

"Mr. Daunois, Dad brags on you all the time. He says you're a very caring man. The Mississippi River levee system has been keeping the river silt from feeding the delta for decades. Dad knows of the problems with erosion of the coast caused by loss of wetlands since the '40s, and this was happening long before the onslaught of....."

"Wait, Lee! Please, I'll ask again? What does this have to do with me? Answer my question, and then we can proceed."

"It's just that I haven't been able to get anybody to listen, nobody who can do anything about it anyway. And now, all the funds and focus are on the spill, so this has gone by the wayside."

"Just what are you saying? Do you want me to help accomplish these things? What in the world has your dad been telling you—that I've got oodles of time AND money?" As Lee nodded, Tarlton continued, "If that's it, he's gone way too far! Believe me; I know all about the canals crisscrossing the wetlands to get to the Gulf of Mexico and how they allow salt water to flow in and kill everything it touches. I know what needs doing. I'm all for what you're proposing, but hear me now, NONE OF IT CAN CRAM INTO MY SCHEDULE!"

"But no one will listen, and it's got to be done. Somehow, with God's help, maybe not everyone along the coast will lose their livelihoods because of the oil. But later on, it'll probably happen eventually anyway, if whatever salvageable wetlands aren't saved."

"Now, let's be more optimistic, Lee. Before the spill, I'd heard things were started along those lines. I have to admit, I'm not up-to-date on it now, but it sounds like you know everything that needs doing. You seem like you've got a good mind for what's necessary and have done your research, so just keep pushing! I really can't help with it."

After having some coffee together, Tarlton walked a calmer and perhaps a more hopeful Lee to his car as Lee shook Tarlton's hand and said, "Thanks for your time," Mr. Daunois, and I'll continue to do what I can. Now, on an entirely different subject, Sir, I've seen Flex at the diner and know a little of his story. I'm a social worker by profession, so I could possibly be of some help if ever it became necessary to locate his birth records."

"Oh, that'd be great. We'd all appreciate that. So far Flex has stayed with Godfrey Gaudin with no legal problems, but I'll surely mention your being willing to help."

"Well, I've taken a liking to Flex too, like everyone, and it's wonderful that Godfrey's taken him in and things are working out for him."

"Thanks for your offer to help, and I wish you the best in your fight against erosion. Give my best to your dad. So long now!"

Tarlton went back into the building intent on tackling the demands of the day. *Nevertheless*, he couldn't completely extricate from his mind Lee's reminder to him of all that needed correcting. He was aware of the past and ongoing wetlands destruction, in addition to the constant nutria damage. Now, the oil spill in the Gulf made things so much worse, it seemed hopeless. Mother Nature built the delta, the river's mouth soil, a long time ago. It worked fine until man messed with it because of a need for oil.

CHAPTER TWENTY-ONE

The following week, during one of the few days she would be at the hospital now, Ilana saved a morning for paint shopping with Amelie, since her volunteer day didn't start until the afternoon. They were enjoying their rare catching-up time together while getting some laughs from some of the weird color combinations available.

"You know, Amelie, I really haven't told you how lovely the Faubourg Marigny is and how nice Tarlton's home is. The colors fit nicely and it's a great area with just about everything within walking distance—book stores, art galleries, cafes. We've even walked to the French Quarter for beignets and coffee and gone to Mass at the cathedral."

Amelie listened, asked the occasional question, and noticed how her mother's eyes sparkled as Ilana continued, "From the second floor of his house, you can see traffic on the river while you hear live music from a nearby bistro. But that's when the windows are open. You know how rare it is to have perfect weather in New Orleans—enough for open windows. But his second floor windows look out over the river, so there are more breezes in summer. It's so lovely!"

"Gee, Mom, it sounds great, hot weather or not. I've heard the Marigny is a lot like Uptown, but with a bit of mystery."

"Yes, I do get that feeling, but mystery in a good way. Homes have been there a long time; you can tell by the mature gardens and the brick sidewalks, which I just love."

Ilana continued her description when they stopped for lunch, "And the Marigny's history that Tarlton's told me about is so interesting too. When you hear that and then go to St. Louis Cathedral amidst its history, it's absolutely wonderful!"

"Mom, I haven't seen you this excited since I noticed how you enjoyed your post-divorce freedom. Are you just in a particularly good mood or could you be wanting to tell me something? Like that you and Tarlton are serious? No, no, wait; I shouldn't ask. It's between you two. I'm sorry."

"Oh no, Sweetie, it's okay really. I am in a great mood because I'm so enamored of him, and I'm realizing our feelings for each other are strong. At least mine are. We spend a lot of time talking, and he listens; he really listens to me." Ilana was suddenly aware that she was feeling like a silly teenager, opening her heart to her daughter as she would've many years ago to a good friend. Emotional as she was, she knew happiness tears would soon fill her eyes if the conversation didn't change direction, so she blurted out, "How's the vet doing? Herb, is it?"

"Oh, he's great, Mom, and by the way, he listens to me too...most of the time. We're going to the Ponchatoula Strawberry Festival this weekend with Addison and Marvel." Ilana looked directly at Amelie as her daughter continued on about fair plans, "Don't you think that'd be great, Mom?... Mom?...Mom, are you listening?"

"Gee, Sweetie, I think I missed the last part of what you said."

"I think you missed it all. Mom, you're not old enough for dementia, are you?"

"No, no, Amelie, I'm fine, just distracted, I guess."

"Are you thinking of Tarlton right now at this very minute? No, I'm butting in again. Shouldn't ask—unless you want to tell me—maybe?"

"Actually," Ilana responded dreamily, "I guess I do, and I WAS thinking of him."

"Oh, Mom, I surely hope you and he are serious because we like him so much."

"Do you? He is a great guy, isn't he? I mean, he's exceptional—with all the good he does—so in tune to others' needs. He always wants to fix everything and make them entirely right. With all he's got going on, he was even asked to help with working on repairing the wetlands, not that he has time for it, but I know he wants to. He's so busy, and so caring, and all the while, such a gentleman."

"Yes, he is—all that," Amelie answered as she handed her mother a napkin, for she noticed the beginning of the happiness tears.

"Oh, I care so much for him and just love how he thinks and what he's able to accomplish. He makes me feel so special and important. He's always telling me that I'm clever and intuitive and even beautiful, and—whether true or not—I sure love it."

Amelie grabbed her mother's hand and squeezed it, "Mom, of course it's true, and you deserve it all, to be treated well by someone who, not only recognizes how special you are but, lets you know it. No one would know it by your tears, but, this might be the happiest lunch we've ever had together in all those we've shared. Now just know that this won't get passed on to Addison. That is unless you'd like me to mention it."

"Believe it or not, I might just like you to—mostly because I know you talk to him often. I don't mind, and anyway, the way I feel right now, I want the whole world to know how happy I am. Oh, but wait, Tarlton and I haven't really said the "L" word. I mean I know he cares, but...."

"Just know how truly happy I am for you," Amelie interrupted, for she could sense the tear flow beginning again. "And I really don't talk to Addison much since Marvel's in his life, so when I see him and Marvel this weekend, her being Tarlton's daughter and all, I probably should stay quiet about it. I really have to go now because I'm meeting the girls at the mall, so I'd better drop you off. You probably should get to the hospital anyway."

"Yes, I surely should," Ilana said as she glanced at her watch. "Let your sobbing mother get herself together a little first." They paid their checks and Amelie watched Ilana dab at her eyes, do a quick lipstick touchup, and take a last sip of iced tea before they rose and left the restaurant.

During the short drive to the hospital, Amelie interjected, "You know, Mom, I'm so glad I've taken my vacation days one at a time like this to be able to see you—I mean, especially now that you're getting busier."

"Me too, Sweetie. Our times together mean a lot to me, and very soon I'll want you to go furniture shopping with me too. If there's time tonight, you could stop by the townhouse before heading home. Tarlton will be coming over."

"Not likely, though I'd like to see him. We'll probably be shopping until closing time and I'll leave straight from the mall to head home. Bye, now. I love you!"

"I love you too, Sweetie," Ilana said as she got out of the car. "Y'all have a great time at the fair this weekend and call when you can. Bye and stay safe!"

Ilana took the elevator up and smiled at familiar faces she passed in the hallways leading to the Intensive Care area. Being here always made her more aware of her good fortune in having her own family and friends healthy. For her own well-being, she avoided allowing herself to show her emotions under these sad, stressful circumstances. Usually it was extremely hard to do, but today she realized a more intense difficulty—that of steeling herself against displaying a far different emotion: joyful exhilaration.

She had revealed, for the first time, her feelings for the special guy in her life, thus experiencing the sheer bliss of facing them herself. Other than a funeral home or graveyard, Ilana couldn't think of a more inappropriate place for her to be when feeling this way. She was happier then she'd ever been, possibly in her entire life, and wanted everyone to know it. *Nevertheless*, as she scanned the updated patient list, she forced herself into seriousness, for she knew she must control too wide a smile when she looked up again.

That afternoon, during some free time, Ilana tried to select colors for Share-Way's outside from the samples she and Amelie had gotten. She soon realized the hospital's fluorescent lighting wasn't conducive to choosing colors that'd be seen in daylight. Ilana knew she must narrow the color choices down somewhat, otherwise the selection process facing her and Amelie would be overwhelming. One of Flex's friends had given her a sketch of the building he'd drawn that she kept in her purse for ready reference. In order to decide, what she needed to do was look at the building with the sketch and paint choices in hand—perhaps from the levee.

The following day was clear and perfect for checking colors by daylight, so with her animal shelter duties complete, Ilana headed to Share-Way. As she reached the area, she slowed to search for a parking spot beside the levee. In one second her rear-view mirror went from being completely void to being swelled with a hood and windshield image like a ball suddenly approaching that she wasn't ready to catch! Stunned by that sight, plus the sound of the blasting horn behind her, Ilana spurred to immediate action—accelerator action.

After driving a while to find a convenient driveway in which to turn around, she ultimately found an appropriate levee-side parking place. Before looking toward Share-Way, she situated herself on the grass about half-way up the levee and directly across from the Share-Way area.

Ilana dreaded looking up and seeing something she knew would infuriate her. If this project, a place that now meant so much to so many, were marred by a used aluminum can, a plastic water bottle, or even something as small as a cigarette—she wouldn't be able to tolerate it. Someone's inability to hold onto something until it could be appropriately discarded was one of the few things that made Ilana absolutely livid, and more so when it was witnessed by youngsters who were then influenced to copy their elders. Why didn't people realize their taxes inevitably went toward keeping attractive the very areas their litter tarnished?

She bravely looked up to thoroughly appreciate seeing the sun shining on what would be the perfect building in the most fitting location—and it was litter free! She breathed a relieved sigh in appreciation as she watched workers measuring, sawing, sanding, and positioning their scaffolds as construction progressed.

With no intention of interrupting any of it, Ilana sat among her paint squares and contrasted them against the building's view as she contentedly listened to the whir of saws from across the road.

CHAPTER TWENTY-TWO

Ilana drove home envisioning yellow flowers on Carolina jasmine or mandevilla vines climbing from either side and over Share-Way's entrance arbor. She could picture Godfrey's wooden benches protected from the rain by the overhang. Best of all, she could even see the yellow Share-Way sign above the doorway.

As she drove into her garage while whispering a thanksgiving prayer that she'd witnessed a completely litter-free Share-Way, Ilana now couldn't believe she'd actually resisted decorating it. Choosing colors and décor for this was TOO IMPORTANT TO MISS being a part of. Anyone would want to help—in any way possible—this place that would become a long-awaited comfortable and secure haven for many.

Ilana entered the townhouse intent on e-mailing the latest Share-Way news to her younger brother and only sibling. She'd been faithfully keeping him updated since its beginning. A career marine who'd traveled everywhere, done everything, and witnessed so many interesting things, he was never easily impressed. *Nevertheless,* he was as intrigued by Share-Way's capacity for correcting obvious problems as about anything she'd ever witnessed, and was always anxious to hear the latest.

How Ilana loved and missed him, the strong, hefty guy who was three years her junior yet surpassed her, both physically and intellectually, very early on. They'd agreed several times in the past to feeling like their ages were somehow reversed. Amelie and Addison dearly loved their Uncle Ib, who'd always been in their lives and never missed a birthday or Christmas with them when they were little. Now, they only talked to him occasionally, usually to thank him for gifts he'd sent that he thought they'd like.

Ilana smiled when she recalled the predicaments she and Ib managed to get into as kids. With Ilana protecting him or Ib covering for her, their mother often used a certain phrase whenever she suspected her two mischief-makers were up to something. She'd say, very mysteriously, "You can feel the undertow," a quote by the spirited heroine in Henrik Ibsen's *Lady from the Sea*. It was her mother's favorite play by the Norwegian poet and playwright, though she'd never been fortunate enough to see any of his plays. Ilana remembered her mother as an avid reader who so strongly related to Ibsen's heroines that she named her son after him.

After finishing a salad while watching the local TV news, Ilana turned on the computer to e-mail Ib, their most convenient way of staying in touch, and discovered an e-mail from him with information for her.

"Sis, I've got some statistics for Tarlton that he may already know about since he's always so on top of things, but I find it astounding. America ranks twentieth of all the developed nations in how we take care of our children, according to a UNICEF study. And I'll bet Tarlton is aware of this too, but it completely threw me to read it. There are 41% more preschoolers of working parents than there are the number of child-care slots."

"Yes, Share-Way is going to partly remedy that," Ilana typed back, "BUT CAN ONLY HANDLE THE SOUTH. Tarlton might not know the exact figures, so I'll tell him."

Ilana played with Blossom a while knowing Ib probably had more to add, and soon on her computer screen was: "I was at a few of the usual-type group homes for some hands-on boy mentoring recently. As I drove away, I made a point of talking to some of the homes' neighbors, and, almost unanimously, they're really unhappy with those homes. The consensus in some areas was that these arrangements are profit-oriented businesses that neglect their properties, pile up trash, and make too much noise."

"I know," she responded, "and some adolescents are put out for misbehaving and left to roam the neighborhoods, which results sometimes in their being involved in felonies. It then becomes their introduction into crime. Thus, innocent lives are ruined."

"I'm so thrilled Share-Way is going to partly remedy this, AT LEAST IN THE SOUTH. I can't wait 'til that thing is completed and I can come in for the grand opening and shake the hand of that special guy of yours. I wish I could have been contributing toward it somehow all along."

"You've done enough by keeping in touch this way. I know I've heard from you way more often since this has come about. You couldn't be helping now, not me anyway, with your lousy color coordination. I'm choosing paint colors for both outside and in. Tarlton's got me choosing colors and furnishings for the lobby too. But the building's looking great already, and I'm proud to do it. Ib, remember when Dad built houses and cabinets and furniture? We were so young, we didn't know what was involved. This is a bigger project than he ever took on, of course, but seeing what's involved makes me appreciate what Dad accomplished much more than I ever did before."

After cleaning the kitchen, Ilana sat down again to see Ib's response: "YOU WERE AROUND A LOT LONGER THAN I WAS, SO YOU OUGHTA KNOW!"

"Okay, Ib. I'm not that much older than you. I can delete you anytime, you know, and I know you're laughing that loud laugh RIGHT now that I love and miss. But honestly, I've got phone messages to handle and more e-mails to get to before bed, but I'll keep you posted. Good night to you with love, you big lug!"

Ilana poured herself a glass of wine, figuring she'd need it, before returning a call from a persistent older Riverside friend. The woman had three sisters living in different states as a result of their husband's career beginnings years ago. Now, as divorcees or widows, they were willing to contribute anything to be Share-Way residents and live together. Ilana understood their missing each other now that they were all alone in houses probably too large for them to handle. Ilana knew the woman merely wanted reassurance—yet another time—that they'd be residents, so even before she could say the reason for her call, Ilana told her, "Now don't you worry. You tell your sisters you're all at the top of the list."

"Have I told you, dear, that we're able to sew curtains to decorate the rooms? And we could teach sewing, and we're willing to do any mending."

"Yes, you've mentioned it, well except the mending part, but I'll include that."

"Thank you, dear. You know I worry about it because I don't have transportation to be stopping in at Share-Way and making sure we're not forgotten."

"I understand. You've told me that too," Ilana tried to say calmly. "Trust me, you and your sisters won't be left out,"

"Oh, thank you so much, dear. I hate to keep bothering you about it, and I'm glad you understand and are taking care of it. It means so much. I'll let you go now. G'night."

They were like so many other women who wanted to contribute any way they could, by babysitting while washing and cooking when the children's parents worked. Many widowers wanted to live at Share-Way and handle any building maintenance and carpentry, as they'd teach the younger residents, both boys and girls. The younger people were interested because they'd heard they'd be taught basic life skills, even though they'd receive no completion certificate. As a result, the resident list was rapidly lengthening.

When Ilana returned to check her e-mails, as she expected, they mostly involved questions from friends who either wanted to be residents themselves or were getting information for others. Actually this was Marvel's responsibility, but Ilana liked having more than the usual contact with people in the area than she normally would've had, so she didn't really mind. She was also beginning to appreciate how easily all involved were working together, for she knew the animosity that could result when employees encroached on the duties of other staff.

CHAPTER TWENTY-THREE

Early the next morning, though not quite her usual rising time, Ilana was awakened by the phone, which she immediately answered after seeing her brother's name and number identified. "Oh goodness, what's happened overnight?" she almost panted. "You never call. Are you all right?"

"Nothing's happened, Sis, but I made a decision I wanted to tell you about right away. I want to pay for all of Share-Way's outdoor area—the benches, tables, the walkways, and landscaping. Now, I know Tarlton's probably ordered all of it already, or at least the material for it, but I want to reimburse him for it—everything for outside. I really feel compelled to do this since I think so much of this idea of his."

"Oh, wow!" she gasped. "Are you sure?"

"Positive! Tell Tarlton I'm insisting on it, in case he objects, and that I'm sending you a check this morning as partial payment and want you to let me know a total cost so I can send more. It'll be my small part in helping Share-Way get started. I possibly could afford the cost of installing a pool also; not quite sure about that yet though. Addison's been telling me how he hoped Tarlton would be putting a pool in. Don't know if I can handle that big expense, but I'd sure like to."

Now that Ilana realized Ib and Addison had been in touch about it all along, she knew Ib must be aware of Addison's interest in being a swimming instructor again. He was also certified as a lifeguard and taught swimming while in college—and loved it.

"He's even told his favorite uncle about a friend who's a qualified instructor," Ib continued. "This friend's concerned about the amount of black kids who don't know how to swim. They both want to teach swimming at Share-Way to help remedy that situation."

Ilana knew as well as Addison that Uncle Ib would be in complete support of that—something else for which there was a definite need. She was certain Ib would find a way for a pool to be forthcoming.

Addison and his uncle were always close, since very early on, and Ilana was sincerely grateful for the positive influence their only uncle had been on both her children. She recalled those two little wide-eyes kids who listened in awe to their uncle's many adventures and admired this interesting man who had an uncanny knowledge of any subject.

"I've got to run now, Sis, but be looking for my check, and tell Tarlton not to take any shortcuts in Share-Way's outside development because I'm covering it all."

"Oh, I can't wait to tell him. He'll be hearing about it first thing this morning. Thank you, and you know I love you—even if you weren't doing this."

"I know and I love you too. I'll be waiting to hear a total cost. Bye."

"Bye, love. I'll call Tarlton right now." Ilana had intended to call Tarlton first thing anyway to relate how impressed she was with Share-Way's outward appearance from the levee. That paled in comparison to this present news of her brother's generous offer. *Nevertheless,* it was all so wonderful, she couldn't wait to tell him everything.

"Hey, I was going to call you a little later," Tarlton said when hearing her voice. "I've got good news and bad news. What do you want to hear first?"

"Good, I guess, and then I've only got good news for you."

"Well, Marvel and I have finally come up with a tentative date for getting all the residents together for a meeting—Thursday after next. Is that good for you? Because I'm not going to proceed with notifying anyone until I'm sure you'll be there."

"That's fine. I know you wanted it to be in the afternoon so I'll get out of volunteer duty starting at lunch on that day. NOW, get ready for my good news! My brother wants to pay for all expenses involving the outside of Share-Way—I mean the pathways you decide on, landscaping, furniture, and even the outside paint. Please let him. This means a lot to him and you could probably use some financial help by now."

"Well, that's fabulous news," and then to Ilana's slight surprise, "I was going to make a loan for that, so it'll be great if he'll be taking care of it."

"Even better than that...you haven't heard the best," Ilana jumped in excitedly. "It seems he and Addison have been talking about a swimming pool and I know he'll pay for that too. Well, he says he'd like to pay for the pool, but I know he will."

"What? Oh, but that'll be way too expensive. I can't believe it. I've so wanted to fit that in but didn't think it would come for a while. Addison will be as happy as I am. He'll be on cloud 9. Give me your brother's number and I'll try to catch him right now to thank him. I really like this guy."

"I've told you, "he's as caring and concerned as you are."

"Oh, Hon, I'm sorry. I'll have to go; a truck's pulling up to deliver something. Really quick, though—I'd like to see you tonight if you can make it."

"Sure, but wait! What's the bad news?" Ilana said quickly while trying to let him get off the phone. "Come over about 6:30, and I'll get with Marvel about the meeting."

"Great, and the news will keep. See you about 6:30."

Ilana called Marvel to set up a time to discuss inviting people over for the next Thursday get-together and Marvel said she'd find some time that very afternoon. Ilana then arranged to get a substitute for afternoon hospital duty and also for animal shelter duty the Thursday of the get-together.

When Ilana arrived, Marvel handed her a complete up-to-date list of Share-Way residents-to-be, along with contact information, for they both knew they'd have to get busy right away with planning this important residents' meeting.

"Marvel, you are just too, too efficient," Ilana exclaimed, to Marvel's delight.

"Thanks, I try, but I've had an on-going list from the very beginning. And you know what? There certainly hasn't been anyone changing their mind. Once they've decided they want to live at Share-Way, they're in for good."

"Oh, that's something really easy to believe. It's just too good a deal to not take advantage of. Whether one's got transportation problems, babysitting problems, lack of skill—whatever, your dad's solving all their problems, and he's a wonder for doing it."

"Yes, he is, and I have to say, I'm surely glad you think so," She gave Ilana a quick hug and added, "And Dad's extra excited now after hearing your brother's news."

"And I really didn't have time to tell him about some things Tarlton might not even have thought of. Let me tell you quick before we get started here. Wouldn't it be extra special to have checkerboard tiled right into the tops of the outside tables—maybe Scrabble boards too? I think your dad said they'll be of a heavy resin or wrought iron.

"Wonderful idea! The residents would love that. And Dad's having these smooth pathways put in made of a permeable substance. Wheelchairs, walkers, and crutches are supposed to be able to manage on it really well, so all ages would have another reason to be out there in that nice seating area under the big oak. You know what? Your brother paying for all this outside enjoyment makes me know he's as special as you are."

"He is pretty great, and he's wanted to help somehow all along because he thinks Share-Way is so needed. I haven't seen him in way too long, so I can't wait for whatever grand opening we might have because he's promised to be here. Now just let me get some coffee, Marvel, and we can get to these necessary things right now."

Marvel joined her in pouring herself a cup of coffee and mentioned, "You know, I hadn't thought about an actual grand opening, but I love that idea, and the time might not be that far away. A lot will depend on this upcoming meeting, in case someone comes up with a problem or something Dad hasn't anticipated, which I doubt will happen. A grand opening celebration surely would be fun—yes indeed—another reason to party!"

The names on the list Marvel compiled all looked familiar to Ilana except a few, so they divided it for contacting purposes, with Ilana planning to see some people before going home that very afternoon. She left in enough time to make the necessary stops, and everyone welcomed her anxiously. They'd all been anticipating a notification of this expected upcoming get-together, after which they could proceed with their moving plans.

The visits completed, Ilana drove to her townhouse planning what she'd fix for dinner. She couldn't wait to see Tarlton, but not this time as usual because she'd fallen so completely in love with him. Tonight it was more because this morning he had dangled the distressing possibility of bad news before her. She'd stayed busy enough all day to keep the thought somewhat at bay, but now had become aware of just how worried she was about the bad news.

Tarlton arrived at 6:30, as planned, and Ilana greeted him at the door with a questioning expression and said, "So?"

Confused, he responded, "What? What's wrong? I'm not late."

"You've had me wondering and worrying all day about your bad news.

I saw Marvel this afternoon and didn't know if I should question her about it for fear of upsetting her...."

"Oh, Gee, Hon, I'm sorry! I did kind of leave you hanging this morning on the phone, didn't I? I don't ever want to do that to you. It turns out... well, let me just tell you about it from the beginning. But first, I'd love a glass of wine, and you look as if you could use one."

"His embrace softened her mood somewhat as she mumbled, "Okay. Geez! Finally I'll get to hear. I'll pour."

Tarlton watched her admiringly as she brought over the wine, and they then settled in comfortably on the sofa and Tarlton began, "Lee called early this morning to say that his dad fell yesterday. He didn't tell me much more than that, except that he tripped on someone's cane at the home. It was one of those four-pronged jobs, you know, with the extensions at the bottom. It seems he stumbled and fell against a wall so didn't fall to the floor, but you'd think he'd been in a nine-rounder if you saw his face. They keep the home's tile floors spotless and almost glistening, so Mr. B didn't notice a silver-colored cane a visitor left close to a chair in the TV room. Of course he's angry with himself for letting it happen. His face took the brunt of the fall, and his shoulder is pretty bruised, along with a rib on that side, so he's hurting and on heavy pain medication."

"But did he know you were there? Did he speak to you?"

"Oh, yes, but by the hardest—he smiled as well as he could when I got close enough to the bed for him to recognize me. His false teeth are cracked so he can't use them. Lee was so glad I'd come, but how could I not be there? Such a wonderful guy, Mr. B is! And Lee's been great in trying to get Flex's adoption arranged and doing whatever possible for the foster-home kids."

"I know. It's because he's so worried they'll get into trouble with drugs and such. And, Tarlton, Lee told me once how bad his dad's vision really is and why. It's macular degeneration he's got, so he can only see through the outer edges of his eyes."

"Well, Mr. B claims he has one good eye, although Lee says that's debatable. His vision's awful, but nobody would even realize it because he manages so well. Anyway, Lee went to get something to eat while I was there, so Mr. B and I were alone for most of my visit. What got to me was that he began talking like he was thinking he might never again get up from that bed. And, by the way, he couldn't speak very well without teeth, and it must be hard for him to talk because his face hurts, but I managed to understand him. He said the birds outside kept chirping something that sounded to him like, 'I miss you—I miss you,' and he thought it might be a sign from his wife. He said there were other times too when he'd heard them chirp, 'you—you—you'... but not like a dove's cooing. He said it was much faster.

"Now don't think that it's the medication doing that, Tarlton," Ilana responded thoughtfully, "because I've heard those same type bird sounds."

"Really? You know, I could swear I've heard things in what the birds chirp too--pretty close to something anyway. I guess you can hear things in the sounds of birds just as people see images in clouds."

"Definitely! I know one of my favorite things is to find time to sit and look at what the clouds form, while listening and imagining what the birds could be saying. Now go on. What else did Mr. B say?"

"Well, after I was there for some time, just sitting bedside holding his hand and trying to be encouraging, he raised his other hand like a sign for me to hush so he could speak. He began telling me how tired he was, not only tired right then, but completely exhausted from the hassle of just living. Oh, Ilana, it reminded me of my mother when it was at the end for her. I was even to the point of imagining a calm coming over him, like with her, a kind of resignation that I believed meant he was ready to go. He said he'd be glad to reunite with his wife and departed old friends. Of course, this was after he assured me that his destination, following his forthcoming departure, would definitely be Heaven.

When Tarlton could tell Ilana was near tears, he grabbed her hand and said, "Wait, wait! Listen to this! Then Mr. B suddenly stopped talking, almost in mid-thought, forced his old feeble eyes to open to full capacity, looked toward me, and asked, 'Tarlton.....you want to come?' And then he burst out laughing, while he clutched his face from the sudden more intense pain, and then said, 'GOTCHA!'

"Ilana, really, he'll be all right, just in pain for a while. I can't believe he did that to me! And I had you going too! Truly he'll eventually be back to normal, the old coot, and just as ready as ever for messing with everyone again, I guess."

CHAPTER TWENTY-FOUR

Once Ilana mentioned that, not only was her brother in an earlier time zone, but that he usually stayed up late, Tarlton couldn't wait to thank him. He quickly punched in the numbers Ilana had written down for him. When Ib answered, he heard, "Man, you either have to be the most generous person in the world or the richest. This is Tarlton and I'm just calling to thank you."

"Well, hey, Tarlton. You're the guy, huh, the one I've heard so many good things about, not only from Ilana, but from Addison and Amelie too. You're so welcome, man. Oh, and there's more. This afternoon I was at the credit union and found out that I can afford to pay for the pool too."

"No! Really? Ilana said you wo...."

"Aw, she knew I'd come across. I decided there'll never be a better use for cashing in some gold coins I bought a few years back. Gold's worth so much more now and I can more than triple my investment. Oh, and I mean for the pool to be protected—a covered one—and, for the residents' convenience, attached to the building. That's if it can still be done at this late date. A covered pool probably should've been figured in your original plan, so I hope it'll work."

"Oh, we'll make it work. Thank you, thank you. We just need to find the most convenient entrance to it from the building. You're sure you can handle it?"

"Oh, yes, and, Tarlton, make sure it's Plexiglas or whatever is recommended for over there, so it can be used all year long. I'm willing to pay any price to have it enclosed with the most storm-resistant material available. I mean it now. Spare no expense."

"Will do. Thanks again. I don't know how you can do this. I've been planning this project a while so was somewhat prepared financially, but you weren't planning on ...."

"I'm just glad I have this opportunity to do some good. My money gets spent on the occasional date and gifts for Ilana and the kids. I've got every electronic, phone, and computer-related gadget, and all the exercise equipment I'll ever need. So, why not?"

"Everyone will be so happy about it. You're the best. I'll put Ilana on. So long!"

Ilana took the phone to say, "You don't realize the people you'll make happy."

"Just keep me posted about it, Sis, and make sure Tarlton gets the very best. Love ya, and I know you need to get some sleep, as I do. It's not every day I commit to spending all this money, you know?"

"I bet not. You stay safe now. Bye, love."

****

Ed was at Godfrey's with some Creole tomatoes from his garden first thing the following morning. "They're really special this year, Godfrey. This is the first batch I've picked and they're beautiful. The reddest ones will be great on sandwiches for lunch."

"Sure, if I don't eat 'em all before then," Godfrey laughed as he spread the greener ones out on the counter for ripening. "Yep, nothin' like our soil for growin' the best."

"And I've got a lot more little ones, if I can just keep the squirrels and bugs and birds away long enough...."

"Uh oh, Ed," Godfrey interrupted as he peered out the side kitchen window. "Here she comes, still in hot pursuit!"

"No, oh no! She wasn't supposed to be around today." When a little time passed and no one knocked, Ed asked, "Come on Godfrey, are you just buggin' me?"

"Yes, he is," Tarlton chuckled as he came into the kitchen from his room.

"Oh, what am I gonna' do about her?" Ed lamented. Y'all know I only mentioned Share-Way to her in the first place because I thought, with her being a retired nurse, she'd be good at Share-Way for giving medical advice. I mean she'd be lettin' the residents know whether to see a doctor and that would be her contribution for livin' at Share-Way."

"We know well your intention, Ed," Tarlton answered, "but it's so darned funny!"

With no encouragement from him, she was attracted to Ed and was convinced they should get married, and, rather than in Share-Way, live in either her house or his. Her unwelcome advances soon became a detriment to his new-found contentment since turning over the diner to his sons. He liked taking life easier now and enjoyed how spontaneous he could be. He and Godfrey looked forward to living at Share-Way, and both chose to stay busy with helping out there.

Like Godfrey, Ed had been a widower for many years and was well accustomed to living alone. Also, like Godfrey, he could never have another woman in his heart, no matter where they lived. As Ed became more frustrated in his inability to make her understand, his current predicament became Godfrey's most enjoyable form of entertainment, and everyone else around couldn't help enjoying it as much.

"Man, I guess you two'll be spendin' time alone out on the benches I'm makin' and I'll have to go fishin' with somebody else."

"Godfrey, cut it out! You know I'm lookin' forward to our goin' fishin' and gardenin' and then cookin' what we catch and grow. I just don't know how to handle this. You should be helpin' me with this instead of givin' me a hard time."

Godfrey laughed as he stood over the kitchen sink eating a tomato, its juice dripping down his elbow.

****

After a wonderful day at another Louisiana festival, this one in Robert, known as the Swamp Pop Music Fest, Addison drove Amelie's date and Marvel home first, since they both lived in New Orleans. Addison and Amelie were to spend the weekend at Ilana's, so the ride there gave them a rare occasion for some sibling together-time.

"So, Mom said you've got your condo up for sale, huh?" Amelie asked since she and Addison hadn't yet spoken of it. "And what's the plan?—to live at Share-Way?"

"Well, at least at first. I'll get all the computers functioning and then start teaching guitar and piano when I have some pupils. And I know your next question is going to be about Marvel."

"You've got that right. How long will you live there? And I can answer my own question. It'll depend how serious you and Marvel are. Well, I've got to say, it's apparent to everyone that your futures definitely include each other."

"Well, Sis, thanks for not making some crack about it, like I expected. It depends how involved we are once Share-Way's up and running. Marvel may stay on because she loves what's she's doing. Regardless, I'd like for us to have a place of our own close by."

They sat quietly a while and listened to the radio when Amelie broke in, "I didn't take advantage of the opportunity we had of Mom teaching us piano. You did! I never paid attention enough to learn the very same things she taught us both. I always preferred singing. Remember, Ad, how I'd make up silly lyrics for the songs you wrote? You were great at writing music—and lyrics."

"Well, imagine that—a compliment from my kid sister! Feeling melancholy and sentimental all of a sudden, are we?"

"It's just something I never have told you—I remembered some of those songs and used them when nothing else would comfort a scared animal. And I used your lyrics, not mine! I guess I miss my big brother sometimes and remember the good times more than the bad. I do know you really have a knack for music. You're so tone-conscious; I bet you could identify the notes of a cell phone ring. You surely did your share of correcting me when my piano playing was off—far beyond necessary, as I remember."

"You know, since we're talking about music," Addison said, while turning the radio lower, "I'll let you in on a secret. I've made up some songs just by listening to Godfrey whistling while he's working or cooking. Did you ever notice how he whistles all the time? It's never a familiar tune, and I know they might be old songs I never heard of. But I follow through with his melody and, you know what? They've given me some pretty good song ideas, and some of them I've put lyrics to."

Amelie was nodding in agreement as she recalled Godfrey's whistling when she said thoughtfully, "I remember your deciding you couldn't rely on music as a career—not enough stability, so you went into architecture. That's my brother—always thinking of the safe way! I really am glad you're finding time to enjoy your music on the side."

"I have to find time for it; it's my relaxation—that and some car maintenance. But, hey, I've liked architecture too. I guess I've got the analytical mind for it. It would be great to teach the guitar to more students other than just Flex though, and it would be kind of a dream come true to be able to write music on the side. And, what about you? Where do you stand with Share-Way or do you want to be involved?"

"Good question. If Tarlton would consent to having horses, I'd love to be training them and teaching horse-riding. So far, the only animals expected, besides the residents' pets, are chickens, cows, and possibly goats, and Godfrey and Ed can handle those. I do love my job dealing with animals and I've also recently become involved with environmental preservation. I don't think I told you anything about that, but I'm really getting into it. So I guess I'm not at all sure of my involvement in Share-Way. It'll depend on just how much of a part animals play in Share-Way's future.

"Let's not forget swimming," Addison blurted out as he suddenly remembered, "now that we know there'll be a pool. I'll be teaching for sure and I know you'd be interested in that too. You did it more summers than I did. No matter what, we're both lucky we've got the option of our present jobs to fall back on, and jobs we like."

"Right!" *Nevertheless*, she was remembering Tarlton's assurance that if he ever decided there'd be horses on the property, she'd be the trainer and horse-riding teacher.

CHAPTER TWENTY FIVE

To all involved, either in its planning or its construction, Share-Way was an exciting undertaking that had demanded cooperation and perfection from everyone, and each one seemed to hold their co-workers to that same standard. They believed in its potential for being of such a benefit to those of all ages, that they gave their all to make it, not only livable, but extremely comfortable. It was very close to completion now and far enough along that potential residents could come together and discuss their personal living quarters and work areas. All had been notified and were on their way to this long-anticipated first-time viewing of their future home.

Tarlton, Marvel, and Godfrey were there all day clearing away whatever would be in the way during the meeting. Flex, after returning from school, was soon put to work vacuuming as Chicory scampered around barking at the vacuum.

Marvel was taking a noticeably long time mixing some punch she planned to put in her late grandmother's crystal punch bowl. This was its initial use since its recovery after Katrina waters came in through levee breaks and ruined so much. Teary-eyed, Marvel was recalling memories of that special lady in her elegantly-furnished home ladling drinks into crystal cups. Knowing Marvel had never been able to bring herself to even unwrap the punch bowl, Tarlton went over and held her while she cried softly. He reminded her of what they both knew his mother would be saying now:

"Use it, my dear, in love and good cheer!"

Marvel could even hear her grandmother saying just that, but with a memorable melodic lilt in her voice that was missing in her dad's rendition. After a while, when able to compose herself, she managed a smile, the smile her grandmother thought the loveliest she'd ever seen, and unwrapped, washed, and filled the bowl.

Ed soon lightened the mood when he entered with a large king cake decorated in black and gold. He proudly proclaimed a fact that somehow got mentioned at every local Mardi Gras gathering: "Just a reminder to everyone—you'll be eating the tastiest king cake around!" King cakes are a Mardi Gras custom normally topped with the traditional purple, green, and gold icing and sprinkle colors—the purple representing justice, green standing for faith, and gold for power. Black and gold were used on this one because Saints football enthusiasm was always in season.

When Ilana picked up her friend who'd been so worried about her and her sisters being residents, the woman got into the car with a basket, saying, "It's sweet of you to be my transportation this afternoon, dear. You don't think anyone will object to my bringing these pralines I made, do you? My sisters and I want to make them weekly, along with cookies, to be sold at the Farmers Market."

"If someone minds your bringing them, there's sure to be someone else willing to eat their share. It's great of you to bother to do it! Everyone loves pralines. And, it's on my way, so of course it wasn't any trouble for me to pick you up."

"Bless your heart. Gosh, I'm so anxious to have my sisters here with me. You can't imagine the loneliness we all feel on a daily basis. I mean, even though we get letters, calls, and e-mails from our children and grandchildren—and even occasional visits—it's the daily routine that's lonely. My sisters will be waiting for my call tonight to report on this meeting. You know what, darlin', we might save a bundle on phone bills too, with this new living arrangement."

"From what I hear, Share-Way might be getting the better of the deal, with you and your sisters willing to do everyone's laundry too."

"Oh no, dear. We'll be happy to do it. We've got a plan for setting up the laundry room clothes bins, and we've put together a labeling and laundry-gathering system. I've been told, everyone has the option of doing their own laundry, though, if they'd rather."

"I can't imagine who'd rather?" Ilana laughed as they pulled in at Share-way.

Flex's foster home buddies were all jumping out of the same old beat-up van, all hoping they'd be able to move into Share-Way. They were willing to mow Share-Way's property, clean the building—inside and out, wash cars, do lawns nearby, and wash windows. Actually, everyone was thrilled with what the artistic ones in the group had accomplished inside the building so far. Besides the lovely lobby mural they'd painted, they'd covered a wall in the gathering/dining area, with a colorful collage of sayings about friendship. What everyone first noticed in the room were phrases like "Love Is Blind, But Friendship Closes Its Eyes" and "Friends Are The Flowers in Life's Garden." When anyone complimented them, Flex informed them proudly that he was the one who discovered their talent.

When Lee Bienvenu came in, the foster home kids immediately gathered around him, for he'd agreed to do what he could to help arrange for their move. Aware of how hopeful they were for it to happen, he'd actually lessened his environmental pursuits to follow through with it and claimed to be making headway.

They were the only ones who knew that Lee had already located Flex's birth certificate, so Lee encouraged them to follow him as he approached Godfrey.

"Here you go, my good man! It's my honor to present you with these papers," and in response to Godfrey's inquiring look, "Within this envelope you'll find a long-awaited birth certificate and instructions on what you'll need to do to adopt Flex."

"Really, Lee? I don't know how to thank you."

"My thanks will be in seeing it happen, and I predict that by the time you're moved into Share-Way, you and Flex will officially be a family."

Godfrey quickly went to find Flex as Lee returned to those he'd brought with him, three elderly gentlemen from the nursing home who were prospective Share-Way residents. His father and their pal, Mr. B, would have been with them, had he not had his recent mishap. All were good-natured, happy-go-lucky guys in phenomenal physical shape for being in their eighties. Two of them were in the nursing home simply because they had no family to help them with their house maintenance and were afraid to trust hired help. Mr. B and another of the gentlemen were there because there'd been a time in the past when they needed more looking after. So far, the four's only contributions to Share-Way would be their Social Security checks, but Tarlton had explained to them that those checks, along with the younger residents' salaries, if managed properly, could allow Share-Way to be self-sufficient.

Lee found the gentlemen enthusiastically discussing some of their new plans with Tarlton, "Now, Tarlton, we're not too old that we can't do some cooking preparation and be counted on to watch a simmering pot," one said.

"Most importantly though," another said proudly, "we want it known that we, along with Mr. B, will be dispensing free encouragement, wisdom, and advice—WHETHER IT'S REQUESTED OR NOT!"

"I'll let everyone know that, gentlemen," Tarlton laughed while shaking their hands, "and it just might be the most important thing said here tonight."

The teenager and his mother from the rental house drove up in a small second-hand car they'd managed to buy. She was extremely relieved they'd be residents, primarily because it meant her son could get back in school. "You know, Sweetie," she told him as they left the car, "I'm mighty glad I'll be able to feel safe when returning from the night library shift to this comfortable and well-constructed place we can call home."

"I know, Mom. I feel better about that too, but could you not call me Sweetie?"

"Oh, okay, Hon, that's probably not a good idea. Oops! I guess 'Hon' is bad too. I'll try to watch it. I'm used to it being just you and me, but now you'll be needed by so many people in your free time. You'll be driving people around for church, appointments, and swimming lessons. We can't let them hear that. Is it okay for me to hug you once in a while?"

"Sure, Mom. I don't mind that so much," he laughed, as they walked in.

Lark noticed them and walked over, saying, "Gosh it's good to see you guys away from that old rent house. I really owe you an apology for not taking better care of the place, and I am sorry. Can we just start fresh? I know you'll be so much better off here."

"Sure, Lark," they both answered, and the mother continued, "I'd like to think you did the best you could, and I hope you and your husband are happy in Houma."

"Oh yes, things are going well for us except that my step-father is so unhappy since I've left. I brought both my step-parents today, but I'm not sure they can be residents. This'll be a great arrangement for you all though, and I wish you the best. I should go help with my dad now. He seems to need constant encouragement."

Lark's step-mother's selling position allowed them to manage well financially, although it kept her away a lot. Her step-dad received a meal daily through the Meals on Wheels program, but he hated not being able to contribute anything worthwhile to society because of his confinement to a wheelchair. In addition, he missed Lark since she'd moved away with her long-lost and found-again love, Frank, the tugboat captain. Lark and her step-mother saw a small but positive change in the step-dad since he'd heard of Share-Way, so all three were hoping this meeting would reveal ways he could be useful again. A large and still strong man, he clutched a short list of possible things he could handle and hoped for input of more ideas that could extend his list.

When Amelie and Addison left the car, they were discussing the forthcoming pool, Amelie possibly more excited about it than Addison. She'd spent more time teaching lessons and life-guarding than he had since she'd attended a local college and was more available for doing it part-time during summers.

They walked into the meeting alongside a woman with a bewildered expression who immediately gained Amelie's attention with, "I just recently heard about this place and a friend told me about this meeting. This seems like the answer to all my prayers. Am I at the right place?"

"Well, this is Share-Way, but most of the residents have been selected."

"Oh no. Is there a possibility of an opening?"

"Maybe. I'm Amelie and I'm somewhat involved; maybe I can help."

"Oh, bless your heart, darlin'! The thing is, I'm having to give up my advertising career—upcoming promotion and all—to stay with my mother full time. We've lived together many years, maybe too many, and she's very dependent on me. I thought if we could live here together, I wouldn't have to quit the job I love. I'm really not a homebody and can't handle being trapped taking care of someone, even my mother. Maybe that means I'm a bad person, but I know I can't deal with it—financially or emotionally.

Amelie took her over to Tarlton as Addison spotted Marvel and walked toward her. Tarlton listened sympathetically as Amelie quickly recounted the woman's story. He said they'd probably find room for her and for her to have a seat with the others. She beamed as she thanked him repeatedly and then found a seat among friendly faces.

As everyone wandered around Share-Way's perimeter, two women came in together, clean and well-groomed, yet in noticeably worn clothes, and then three others, each holding a toddler's hand. All needed babysitters, although two had found someone to keep their children while they attended this meeting. One was a licensed hair stylist, another a manicurist, and all were in similar unfortunate circumstances involving dead-beat husbands who'd left them with no child support or transportation. Two others held minimum-wage jobs but were determined to learn a skill, one to become a decorator, and the other a court reporter.

"Girls, who do you think is in the worst fix of all of us?" one asked as they found seats together. "My subbing at the only school I can walk to is just not getting my bills paid. I haven't told y'all, but I've been dodging my landlord."

"Well, I don't know who's got it worse, but all I know is there's only so much clothes to be ironed in return for my getting babysitters for my kids."

Another added, "This definitely is our last hope— to live here, share babysitting, and somehow get some transportation." They held hands as they did each time they were reunited, for they were too far apart to help each other, except by phone encouragement.

Addison and Marvel sat down in front of them as Addison overheard the word, 'transportation,' and quickly turned to say, "No worries—one of my duties is handling some of the transportation. Another guy and I are doing it. We can work out a schedule so one of us can get you to your jobs or classes."

"Really?" came from all of them at once, and "Wonderful! Oh, thank the good Lord!" There would've been tears at that point, but they'd been forced to develop inner and outer toughness, so emotions tended to remain muted in their hearts and throats. *Nevertheless,* one looked all around and said, "And we'd have this great place to live in! Oh happy day! You do know we're willing to do anything—all the cleaning and ironing around here, and anything else needed, don't you?"

"We know," Marvel answered sympathetically. "We'll work it all out fairly for everyone, so that no one's expected to do more than their share. Don't you worry."

CHAPTER TWENTY-SIX

When everyone had spent a sufficient amount of time checking out the building and getting their bearings on where things were, appropriate rooms were chosen. All rooms had neutral colored floors of eco-friendly linoleum, and vertical window blinds were soon to be installed. Residents had the option of covering the floors with rugs and the windows with curtains. *Nevertheless,* all were pleased with the bare floors and the privacy the blinds would provide, plus the added advantage that, being vertical, they wouldn't collect dust. They were given cards containing their room dimensions to figure furniture placement. Wall paint swatches and window blind samples were also provided, from which they could make their choices.

Tarlton announced there were willing volunteers in Riverside who owned small trucks and could handle moving the locals in. A larger truck was also available for moving any cumbersome things like the requested exercise equipment anyone owned. "Now, I've been anxious to tell you about a new development, something that wasn't to happen here for a few years. Because of a generous benefactor, namely Ilana Hayes' brother, Ibsen Hayes, an enclosed swimming pool will be incorporated into our building construction here at Share-Way."

After elated cheering, Addison played a CD to get their attention and he began, "Now, if any of you have long-forgotten tapes or phonograph records that you've stored away, please bring them. I can make them into CDs that all can enjoy. If you have musical instruments, please bring them also. Of course, I'm warning you, those residents with instruments might be asked to entertain at some point in the future," he laughed as he turned the floor back over the Tarlton.

"I must discuss something with all of you before I let you leave, but you should get to know your future housemates—possibly long-time ones. We'll let you have your visiting and getting-acquainted time now, during which you'll also be expected to let Marvel know if you'll need moving help and to confirm anything you should follow up on. We'll have to get your attention again in a bit though for something I consider most important."

About an hour went by when Tarlton had Addison start a CD playing "The National Anthem," which got the group's attention again. At its conclusion, Tarlton began, "Friends, I guess you know this undertaking has demanded cooperation from everyone involved who believes in Share-Way's potential. We've done our part, and now expect you to live here in a spirit of support, congeniality, tolerance, and, as the name implies, sharing. Therefore, some things must be understood and thoroughly agreed upon for this living arrangement to work cohesively. This is a serious matter because anyone not agreeing to the following conditions will not be accepted as a resident. Please give me your complete attention and do speak up with any questions when I've finished. Now, here goes…."

"At Share-Way there will be no complaints regarding another's beliefs. One's right to believe in NO higher power will also be respected. Should a religious service or prayer group be started, anyone not wanting to hear it will be expected to leave the area or use ear plugs. Should someone be in attendance for a meal who is prohibited from eating certain foods, he or she would be expected to eat from the meal what their beliefs allow. Food will not be specially prepared for any guests, but their hosts would have the use of the kitchen for preparing a quiet meal for them.

"Domesticated pets will not only be allowed, but encouraged, but there will be no wild pets. Friendly and house-broken dogs will be given free reign of the building, as long as no one develops an allergy to them. Should an allergy problem arise, owners are expected to be sympathetic and accommodating, to the point of retaining those pets in their rooms. Cats and birds will be kept in their owners' rooms at all times because neither can be controlled. They can and will get on any surface, whether an eating or food-preparation area, thus must be restricted."

When Ed heard this from the kitchen, he had to stifle a yell while trying to whisper, "Alleluia! That's it! Godfrey! That's my out!" She's got cats and they go everywhere in the house. She won't be able to live with that rule! She'll have to stay where she is! Alleluia!" He hugged Godfrey out of sheer excitement.

"The cats rule doesn't solve your problem. She wants to be at your house or hers!"

"I can't live with cats! That's my out! I'm not livin' with 'em!"

Tarlton continued, "There will be birthday parties and other celebrations, if wanted by the one being celebrated, and they can be as extravagant as manageable. During Christmas season, Christmas music will be played. Second line and carnival music will be played during Mardi Gras. On patriotic holidays, "America the Beautiful" or "The National Anthem" will be played. Finally, EVERY DAY somewhere on the grounds, there will be an American flag.

"That concludes what I consider a list of very important terms. Please think about them and assure yourselves you're in total agreement. If anyone, after truly pondering these conditions deep in his or her heart right now, cannot agree to them, I'm sorry to have to tell you....THAT'S A DEAL BREAKER!"

All was quiet, except for sporadic mumbling, until someone yelled, "Fine by me!" and another hollered, "Seems fair enough!" Everyone soon nodded their heads in agreement. Tarlton thanked them for coming, at which time all cheered. Some walked around more, asked questions, and finalized moving arrangements. They then gradually said their goodbyes and headed toward their vehicles.

****

"The pool should go in back to be away from the road and river," Tarlton said to Ilana as he locked the building. "And it'd probably be best on the southwest side."

Ilana was distracted and didn't answer for she'd noticed Addison and Marvel leave together but didn't see Amelie. She wondered why Amelie wasn't with them since Addison was to bring her home. Addison knew his mother so well that he clued Marvel in on her thoughts, and, before she could ask, he said, "Amelie's with Lee, Mom."

"Yes, Ilana," Marvel said, "Amelie went with him to bring some foster kids back to the home, maybe the same kids who stayed to tell me they'd be here every day after school to paint the rooms. Amelie and Lee seemed to hit it off too. Amelie's impressed at how Lee's so driven about saving the wetlands and what he's doing for the foster kids."

A relieved Ilana answered, "It'd be perfect if Lee loves animals too."

"Don't know about that, but from what I saw, Lee seemed very interested in her!"

"Gee, and he seems like such a nice guy too," Addison said sadly. "Too bad!"

"Oh, Addison! Now that I think of it, their interests should blend well."

"Dad, I should mention, before I forget," Marvel said. "The kids who are going to do the painting do have one condition. They want Chicory kept away from here when they're here with paint."

"Done!" Tarlton answered. "Flex'll be willing to do that. Gee, I wish all problems were solved that easily."

CHAPTER TWENTY-SEVEN

Ed and Godfrey said their goodbyes to everyone as Godfrey gave Flex the house key, along with instructions to get ready for bed, "with no messin' around."

When Godfrey turned back toward him, Ed blurted out emphatically, "I'm just gonna' tell her…I'm doin' it!…Heck, I gotta do it!!"

"I've known you so long that I know you won't be able to," Godfrey answered as he put his arm over Ed's shoulder. "You just don't know how to handle a woman like her—not that I do either, so I can't say I can help—but I'm willin' to, if you need me."

"She's relentless, Godfrey. She called this mornin' wantin' me to have lunch with her. I had to make up all kinds of excuses without tellin' her about this meetin', so she wouldn't show up here. Now, of course, she wants me to have lunch tomorrow."

"Oh Lordy! Well, I guess you had to agree to go, so would it help if I were there with you? You know, to back you up when you say, 'No way'!"

"Man, I might need a whole army!"

"I've got to get in with Flex," Godfrey answered laughing. "Let's you and me go to her house tomorrow, before lunch, and you tell her. Okay?"

"Okay! I might as well try. I mean I have to!"

The next morning after Flex left for school, Godfrey walked over to Ed's house without a clue as to how Ed's lady friend could be approached. As he walked in, he was surprised and more than pleased to find "lover boy" resolutely resigned to taking care of the situation.

"I'm callin' her now to say we'll be over in a bit, Godfrey. I've had it with her!" He picked up the phone, then replaced it again, did that a couple times, and finally pressed the buttons. After a very short conversation, he hung up the phone, looked at Godfrey sternly, and said triumphantly, "Well, we're on! By lunch time, if all goes well, she'll be completely out of the picture, so you'll be havin' to get your kicks somewhere else."

It was a quiet ride over to her house, in which time Godfrey realized he'd watched his friend go from mere aggravation, to intense aversion, and finally now to complete disgust, so he could only figure that at this point, Ed was a driven man!

Ed pulled into her driveway from the direction that put Godfrey closer to her carport. An exaggerated toothy smile greeted them as she graciously came out her side door. Ed stormed from the truck, slamming its door with his full force, and approached her staunchly.

"Eunice, there's somethin' I need to say. I'm gonna' say it only once. Understand me completely, because I don't want to hear any guff about it! I'm turnin' my house over to my grandson who's goin' to chiropractor school. He'll move into my house and use whatever furniture I leave in it. I won't be needin' it because ... I'M MOVING TO SHARE-WAY!...End of discussion!"

"But, Darlin', I thought we could be together in...."

"We can't be ANYTHING! And don't be callin' me Darlin!"

Godfrey watched an Ed he'd never seen before abruptly turn away from her and return to the truck. He slammed the door with the same amount of force as before, buckled his seatbelt hurriedly, and started the engine.

A bewildered Eunice implored through the passenger side window, "But what about?...Why?...What?"

Godfrey answered slyly, "You and your cats wouldn't be happy at Share-way. So long now," and Ed quickly sped off.

"Whoo, boy!" Ed yelled, "I feel great! I did it, and didn't give her a second to argue. Wow! I feel like an anchor's been lifted off me. Man, that felt good!"

"You were unbelievable! I'll miss seein' you squirm when she comes around though, but you made it final enough! She WON'T be comin' around."

They rode a while, laughing as the radio blared until they were almost to Godfrey's. Ed then lowered the radio and said, "Thanks, I guess I owe you. You musta given me the push I needed." He soon turned the radio off and said, "Now, buddy, I think you need a push."

"What? For what? I don't have any women runnin' after me!"

"I know, Godfrey. It's your house." Ed drove into Godfrey's driveway, turned the motor off, looked at Godfrey and said softly, "I've been lettin' you have your fun with my Eunice problem 'cause I knew you were havin' a hard time about movin', but you gotta do it. It's hard for me too, but my stuff's stayin' in my house. You know after my grandson's been livin' in dorms, he'll move in with nuthin'. And Tarlton said you can leave anything you want to in your house, and he won't even paint it, since you kept it up so well. You always ignore it when he brings it up, so if you havent' heard, he promised he won't ever tear it down, and you can go in it anytime you want. Godfrey, he even wants you to feel like you can go back to livin' there if Share-Way doesn't work out for ya."

"I know. I did hear him when he said all that. I just didn't want to think about it. And you're right. I need to do it. I've just been puttin' it off. There are just so many memories in there." His eyes watered as he quickly wiped his face with his sleeve. "I can even picture her at the sink, or sittin' on the sofa, or at the table across from me havin' coffee. She loved this place and our garden. Oh, so many years here…"

In a valiant yet clumsy effort to change the subject, Ed interjected, "You know what I forgot to tell you, pal? As payment for my house, my grandson is offerin' you and me chiropractic adjustments. Now I won't be the one needin' 'em, but you surely will."

"Ha, you'll be the first one on his table after we get finished doin' all our vegetable plantin'—you'll see how right I am about that!"

"And, Godfrey, you know I'll help you with the move in any way I can."

"Oh, I know and I know it'll work out and it's for the best. I just gotta' do it, and soon. Tarlton wants to make the house into some sorta cottage garden house for storin' outside equipment. If I'm out soon enough, Ilana's brother might consider coverin' that expense too."

"Seems like plenty enough reason for you to get on it! You and me need to really get serious, and I mean NOW, about gettin' moved into our NEW digs!"

That very afternoon, Ed made his second important phone call of the day—to Ilana. He knew she'd be the best one to encourage Godfrey, plus he'd remembered that, not that long ago, she'd left the home where she'd raised her kids, so she'd be able to relate to what he was going through. Ilana agreed to be over at Godfrey's that coming Saturday morning and called Tarlton to make sure he'd be free and his truck available.

She thought it necessary yet bold on her part, *nevertheless* Ilana contacted Godfrey's daughters to discuss their father's move. They both agreed to talk to him about the furniture they'd like, and planned to be there Saturday with boxes for hauling china and kitchenware.

Since the beginning of construction, Godfrey had agreed to what they envisioned for his house: a storage/sitting/resting area. Therefore, the furnishings to stay would be the sofa, bookcases, storage units, kitchen appliances, dinette table, and all chairs.

By Saturday morning, Godfrey had what he'd bring to Share-Way in one section of the house and was as ready for the move to happen as he could be. Tarlton came into the kitchen, put his arm around his shoulders, and said, "Now, Godfrey, are you going to get all mushy on us today? Remember, you told me once that your wife was the sentimental one?"

"I always thought she was, but some things get to me. If I'm bein' too much of a softy about this, I hope you'll make sure everyone knows I realize it's only a structure."

"That I would do, if I thought they didn't already know that. Trust me. They all understand."

Before long, everyone arrived, ready and willing to pack, wrap, carry, move, or push, a sweet man's possessions into a new future. When they all stopped to lunch on some sandwiches Ed had brought over, Godfrey pointed out where his wife had marked and dated their daughters' growth rates. Then, in another room, he showed them where he'd done the same for Flex.

To lighten the mood, which at this point had the potential of becoming somber, Ilana interrupted. "I'll bet there are some things you don't likely have in this house, Godfrey. I know there are no windows that've been repaned after being broken by balls, or busted screens, or wall holes where a bench press session went wrong."

"Nope, I gotta say, there's none of that here. I guess because ours were girls, and really girly girls too."

"Oh Godfrey," Ilana sympathized as she went over and hugged him, "just be content knowing that all those years this house sheltered a family headed by two caring parents. And the love you all share will always include one who now shares it in heaven."

"Yes, Dad," one daughter said, "we need to remember that!" as both daughters went over and hugged him, while all three cried together in memory of someone special.

CHAPTER TWENTY-EIGHT

After an exhausting but fulfilling moving-out day, Godfrey repeatedly thanked those who'd helped and were now heading for their cars, "I really appreciate your time and effort. Now y'all get some well-deserved sleep."

"Ilana and I will be here in the morning after church," Marvel said as she hugged everyone goodnight.

"Yes," Ilana added, "we're planning to get in there again and clean all the cabinets and storage units really well before other things go in them—that is, now that we've removed all your memories out of there, Godfrey, so you can take them with you."

"That I will! And you know what? I'm feelin' pretty good about it. Now we can go on to the next step. Tarlton, if maybe you, Ed, and I could decide exactly what will be stored in the garage, I could get started buildin' some shelves in there tomorrow."

"Man," Ed countered as he grabbed Godfrey around the neck, "Will you quit findin' stuff for me to do? Right now, let's just hit the sack at my place, since we've run you out of yours."

As Godfrey, Tarlton, Flex, and Chicory walked toward Ed's to spend their first night of temporarily bunking there, Godfrey said through a yawn, "I'd sure like to find the leaves to the dinin' table, so we could make the table bigger. We've been through the house enough today to have run across 'em, so they must be in the attic. Ed, you musta helped me put 'em up there, so I wish you'd help me remember."

"Godfrey, I don't remember where they are. I can't remember where things are in my own attic. Now, if you'll just quit tryin' to keep me busy, I promise I'll fix us some eggs, bacon, and giant biscuits for breakfast in the mornin'. And if anyone's hungry now, please help yourself to anything you find in the kitchen."

"I'm gonna get a peanut butter sandwich and some milk before bed," Flex said as they entered Ed's house, "and I'll be ready for breakfast whenever you're cookin' it. Y'all sure worked me today! I'm as beat as when I play catcher in a ballgame in the heat."

"Oh, but we've gotten so much done," Tarlton told Flex as he turned to look at Godfrey. "We've actually changed a life—Godfrey's. And I'm hoping, more than anyone, that we've changed it for the better."

"I have a hunch you have," Godfrey answered thoughtfully. "And I couldn't be more pleased with what you've got planned for the house and what you've already done with the carport."

Godfrey's double carport was now enclosed, with the doors opening toward each other instead of rising. They now also faced the side instead of the front to make the garage more easily accessible. This gave the house an entirely different look, *nevertheless,* one Godfrey thought very attractive—the look of a garden house.

"I'm also excited about an idea I haven't told y'all about yet. Want to hear about it now?" Godfrey asked, looking at Ed, yet knowing his response.

"Not me," Ed answered while adamantly shaking his head. "I'm off to bed, but, Tarlton, just know Godfrey'll be happy as long as he's finding things to keep him busy, and for some reason, he always wants to include me. Now Flex, you'll have to take the den sofa, well because you're the smallest, and it'll put you closer to the door for lettin' Chicory out in the mornin'. Oh, and you'll find some dog food in the bottom cabinet.

Tarlton, you and Godfrey have the twin beds in the room down the hall. Godfrey'll show you. I'm whipped! G'night all!"

While Godfrey and Tarlton waited for Flex to take a quick shower, Tarlton asked Godfrey to fill him in on his idea.

"It's for some dollhouses for the Share-Way kids. I could build two or three and we could put them on one of those road rugs that kids play with cars on."

"I love that idea! I was wondering what we could put in a corner of the gathering room for the kids. We'll make it a little play neighborhood. The kids would love it. It might be hard for you to manage those tiny pieces with your arthritic hands though. You never mentioned it, but the purple martin birdhouses must've been a struggle for you. You could surely teach whoever's interested how to do it and we could buy the little furniture for the houses."

"You know, I built dollhouses for my daughters when they were little," Godfrey reminisced, "and I remember my wife makin' doll clothes for their dolls. Maybe some residents would be willin' to sew up some doll clothes."

"Godfrey, Ilana says some women are seamstresses. I'll bet they'd be more than willing."

Marvel and Ilana showed up the next day as promised and started right in on vacuuming and wiping all places to be used for storage. Both were relieved on this sunny Sunday that enough had been accomplished the previous day to make only a good general cleaning all that was necessary. Everything they intended to move out was now gone, leaving only Godfrey's personal things he'd be taking to Share-Way.

"So, Ilana, Amelie and Lee are dating now?" Marvel asked as she climbed a ladder, "although I hear it's more like they're doing heart-wrenching things together now, things like cleaning up after the Gulf oil spill. I'm not sure that counts as dating."

"All I know is they've been removing the oil from the birds and she's been able to bring cages from the research lab to keep the poor things in. She says it's important to get all the animals cleaned off as soon as they're oiled. They've also gotten involved now with taking care of the baby turtles that are so threatened—the Kemp's Ridleys and the Hawksbills, I think she called them. It seems the small turtles, those less than two years, can't swim to the really deep water to escape the oil like the older ones can. Releasing them on the Texas coast is the plan, and all are hoping it's a wise decision."

"Well, God bless them for doing such hot hard work, and it's awful that their efforts will be needed for a long time to come. I've read that only some of the oil has been recovered after the Exxon Valdez catastrophe years ago because the cleanup is so difficult. And it's so much worse here."

"I guess you haven't seen Addison much, since he's helping them on weekends."

"I haven't seen him in way too long, and I surely miss him, but we talk often and text. I'm glad he's helping though, but he's been so frustrated, like everyone, with BP, the Coast Guard, OSHA, and government red tape. Nobody would listen to the locals' recommendations on what should be done to prevent further damage. So much clean-up wouldn't have been necessary, had they been heard. I do tend to be somewhat more vocal about my frustration than Addison, and I can get pretty riled up about it if I think about it too much. How could the oil industry get by with drilling that deep with hardly any regulations or accountability? They apparently had insufficient inspection procedures and no plan of who'd be in charge should there be a problem." She sat on a ladder rung, took some deep breaths, and continued, "Oh, I can't let myself get upset about it again. I just miss him so much. EVERY WEEKEND HE'S THERE—doing his part with the others—in that awful heat, fighting the oil."

"And that's a shame. I mean that romances have to suffer too. The ruination of parts of the Gulf Coast is enough, with the jobs and livelihoods lost, some of them permanently I'm afraid. Relationships shouldn't have to be jeopardized too. I've been so thrilled both my children are in wonderful developing relationships! You know how I feel about you already, and now I'm finding that Lee's such a compassionate guy, about the wetlands and now the wildlife. Amelie cares a lot about him. The guys she's dated, it seemed, were way too self-centered or career-driven for her."

"You do know that he arranged to get Flex's buddies into Share-Way before he let himself get so completely involved in saving whatever can be saved out there?"

"Yes, your dad told me. Isn't that the best?"

"And, even with all he's been doing, he's insisted on being counted on to help get Share-Way residents moved in as he promised? He called to tell me that yesterday."

"Really? What a great guy! But his dad doesn't know what he's been doing. He only knows he doesn't come around to see him enough. Since all this oil spill news would be way too heartbreaking for the residents, they've kept TV news off completely at the home. I've gone to see him a few times to make sure he had what he needed and that his things were in order and ready for moving. He's anxious to get moved in but keeps wondering about Lee. He knows of Lee's concerns about the environment, so he usually knows what worthwhile cause he's helping with. This time he doesn't."

CHAPTER TWENTY-NINE

What transpired during the following decision-making weeks was exactly what one would expect when a large home is nearing completion. Tarlton's inspection and approval of everything were required and the workers wouldn't have wanted it any other way for they took great pride in their contributions to Share-Way. Tarlton's demands for perfection had been apparent from the very beginning, and his high standards influenced the workers, who in turn expected the best from each other on a daily basis.

The finishing touches were steadily being accomplished: ceiling fans hung in rooms where they'd been requested, final painting touch-ups made, blinds installed, and floors laid. Small trucks could be seen driving up to the entrance daily as residents gradually moved their possessions into their okayed rooms. The three-foot-wide doors, installed to accommodate wheelchairs, had the added advantage of allowing furniture to be moved through them easily. Everything was put into their specified places, and then, as usually happens with placing furniture, inevitably rearranged to supply more comfort or function.

Soon after the installation of the lobby flooring, Ilana's furniture selections arrived, with only a minimum of delivery confusion. She'd been surprised by the amount of choices to pick from and felt confident in what she'd chosen, but knew she couldn't completely relax about it until she saw everything in place.

Furniture purchases had been minimal, as it turned out though, once Tarlton mentioned some of his mother's furniture was in storage. He had salvaged some valuable pieces from her home, the contents of which had been ravaged by eight feet of Katrina's water. Following the horror of facing it all when removing them, he'd gotten on a long list of people wanting their recovered furniture cleaned. After that was finally accomplished, he'd stored them, and only saw them again when he opened the unit again to bring the furniture to be checked for possible refurbishing.

Ultimately, only the mahogany pieces—a curio cabinet, a hutch/credenza, and three end tables—were deemed worthwhile, so they were the only pieces refinished. When the process was complete, Ilana went with Tarlton to see the redone pieces.

"Oh, Ilana, the difference between the BEFORES, as I remember them, and the AFTERS, when seeing them now, is astounding!" he exclaimed at seeing the results. "I'm sure Mother would've been more than pleased!"

"They are beautiful, Tarlton. There's no doubt! But I have to tell you, I'm worried about my selections meshing attractively with these lovely older pieces. It's been my experience that the way things appear in another location doesn't always turn out to look as I've imagined when they're put in place."

The appointed delivery day, Tarlton, Godfrey, Ed, Marvel, and a very anxious Ilana watched the lobby gradually develop as a piece of furniture at a time was placed amidst the loveliest of marsh murals. When everything was in position and the lobby's overall impact became visible, Ilana allowed herself to exhale triumphantly. She almost screamed, "Oh, it's wonderful! It's much better than I expected! I have to say it myself, This is absolutely stunning! Oh, Tarlton, I didn't have the pleasure of knowing your mother, but she would've had to approve of her furniture used this way."

"Yes, definitely, Mother would've loved it and loved you for showcasing her furniture so splendidly. But I do recall a time, not that very long ago, when you thought you couldn't handle it. Remember that?"

****

One morning as Godfrey and Ed joined Tarlton in the gathering area, Godfrey asked, "Tarlton, with all this you've provided for entertainment, do you think any chores will ever really get done around here?"

"Well, I have to admit, I do fear someone will discover something I've omitted."

Share-Way's huge gathering room held a large TV in one corner for playing Wii games. Heavy, yet moveable, tables for four were scattered around for playing cards and board games on. Long church pew benches lined the corner of the room that housed a ping-pong table. Another benched corner space bordered a shuffleboard court that Flex's artist buddies had painted on the floor. A pool table filled the room's center, a position that supplied ample elbow room, and flat wall cabinets held pool table and shuffleboard equipment. The cabinets were another example of Tarlton's forethought, for these would keep things off the floor and avoid accidents.

"Tarlton you've really thought of everything," Ed added. "GODFREY'S KEPT ME SO BUSY, this is my first time to see everything. I just noticed the small rooms with sofas, and they each have a private bath too. Those are great for anyone just wanting to sit and have a quiet drink or read in silence."

"That too, but they're mostly for overnight visitors, and the sofas you see are sofa sleepers. The rooms can also be get-together areas for smaller groups."

"You really have thought of everything," Godfrey interjected. "I didn't know those were sofa sleepers. And if I know Ilana, she'll make sure the linens are right there handy in each room's closet. Ed, I don't know about your being SO busy. You spend a heck of a lot of time outside in the shade on those benches under the big oak."

"Hey, you're usually there with me, if I recall."

"You know guys, I'm so glad the benches were delivered in time for the workers to enjoy them. And once the pool stonework and the landscaping are complete—and I hesitate to say it out loud—we'll be done!"

After another satisfying day of seeing things successfully coming to an end, someone discovered that the outside trim's final coat of paint was dry. This initiated suggestions of where the Share-Way sign should go. Tarlton, of course, after consultation with Ilana and Marvel, had decided much earlier on its location, and the sign was ceremoniously erected that very evening. That symbolic gesture, so special to everyone involved, was reason enough for a party. Excellent music was provided by Addison's CDs and snacks were brought in, courtesy of Ed's Diner, as all toasted the yellow SOUTHERN SHARE-WAY sign on the building's front.

****

With her decorating responsibilities completed, Ilana returned to her volunteer work schedule. She'd anticipated Tarlton's being extra busy during these final weeks, so had taken on a full work-load herself, but it somehow didn't keep her busy enough to prevent her missing him. They'd gotten into a routine of seeing each other daily at Share-Way and then having dinner together at her townhouse almost every night. The rare times now they did meet, she found herself wondering about instances of slight evasiveness on his part. She knew she had an annoying habit of analyzing things entirely too much, so she tried to brush it aside as merely that. However, the instances that currently concerned her tended to do nothing but augment her current unshakeable lonely feeling.

Amelie's environmental assistance prevented her being with her mother for the usual together times—occasional lunches and spontaneous phone conversations. She normally heard from Addison weekly; it had been way too long since that had happened.

Driving home one evening after an extra tiring day at the shelter, in addition to the usual exhausted feeling, she felt empty. The appreciation of the shelter dogs always seemed obvious to Ilana, thus making her volunteer efforts worthwhile, for she firmly believed animals felt and showed emotion. *Nevertheless*, that day she realized more than usual how much she needed Blossom's instant greeting when she opened the townhouse door. There she was, immediately at Ilana's feet, as expected, in loving enthusiasm, ready for the slightest greeting without any demand of reciprocation.

"Oh, I'm especially happy to see you too, Blossom. Do you know how lonesome I am and how much better you make me feel? I know they're all doing really good things now, but I miss them so much. How about if you and I go for a walk before dark and then come back for something to eat and then some TV watching?" Blossom's tail responded eagerly as Ilana put down her purse, changed her clothes, and got the leash. "And you know, if your little Violet hadn't turned into such a sweet-natured dog, Amelie wouldn't have had so many people willing to keep her now. It would've been great to have your daughter back here for a reunion, huh?" *And the added activity in here would have been a wonderful distraction for me too,* she thought. Ilana sensed a deeper appreciation of her devoted companion as she attached the leash and closed the door behind them, for she realized Blossom's presence meant she didn't have to enjoy the dusk alone.

When dusk had eased into night, forcing their return to the townhouse, Ilana filled Blossom's food and water dishes, and sat down at the computer with a sandwich and some iced tea. An e-mail from Ib wasn't unusual so Ilana had begun to expect one almost every night now, but this particular night's e-mail from him brought her instant delight. It read; "Sis, I just can't wait to see everything, so I'm flying over there this coming week as soon as I can get a straight flight. I'll rent a car at the airport to have wheels while there. I won't be able to surprise you since I'll need some directions as to where your new townhouse and Share-Way are."

Ilana immediately picked up the phone and called him. "I'm so excited. You big lug, you know I can't wait to see you! I've got an extra bedroom here, so stay as long as the marines can manage without you!"

"Well, I'm thinking I could be there for possibly a week and a half. I've been trying for a while now to tie up some loose ends so I could come, and I'm finally making some headway."

"Wonderful! We'll all be thrilled to see you, and I'm so anxious for you to meet everyone. Now, for directions: If you show up any week-day, just cross the bridge and get on River Road. Then come to Riverside and start looking for a large building set toward the back with a beautiful yellow 'Share-Way' sign above the main entrance. Someone's always there during the week. Getting to my townhouse would take more explanation. This way will be much easier. Call me when you're on the ground, and if it's after hours, I'll meet you at Share-Way."

"Great! I'll e-mail you my flight information. But quick, how're things going?"

"Well, everyone's just about moved in. Landscaping is getting finished. The pool is complete except for the surround's sealing and such."

"I don't know, Sis. Is something wrong? Somehow you don't sound as excited as I thought you'd be at this point."

"Oh, I'm mostly just lonesome. I don't see Addison and Amelie like I used to since they're so involved with the oil clean-up, and it's been a time-consuming few weeks for Tarlton." Suddenly, with no advanced warning, Ilana felt her throat tighten and immediately knew what that meant as she sensed tears starting. She tried her hardest to swallow her sobs as she quickly said, "I've got to run now. Love ya. Bye."

"Hold on! Wait! Hold up! Don't hang up when you're upset. What's going on?"

"Oh, geez, I can't ever hide anything from you, even now. It's true. I don't see them enough, but Tarlton seems distant in the few times I do get to see him lately. And I know he's got a lot on his mind now, but he usually shares everything with me."

"Sis, it's understandable Tarlton wouldn't want to go over it all again when he sees you, after he's been dealing with it all day. You're probably his break to look forward to and get away from it."

"I know, but I can't help feeling he's hiding something. Ib…I feel an undertow!"

He laughed so hard, he could hardly stop, for it'd been so long since he'd heard that. "Oh my, that brings back so many Mom memories. Now trust me, Sis. It's probably nothing, but if you're still insisting something's wrong by the time I get there, we'll handle it together. Don't you be worrying and over-analyzing everything like you always do. Now calm down, blow your nose, and go to bed. You just concentrate on your volunteer work and you'll be okay. I'll see you soon. Love ya, Bye."

Ilana hung up and, as soon as she'd pulled herself together, called Tarlton to ask, "Do you think we could start planning Share-Way's grand opening some time in the next week and a half? Ib's coming in!"

"Oh, that's great! Sure, let's do that! I'll have Marvel get right on it. We could do it next weekend. Hey, can I come over sometime soon, like tomorrow night? It's really been way too long since I've seen you. I can't even remember when it was. It must've been an eternity ago. Seems like it anyway."

"That's really very sweet, since it's only been three days. I'll be at the jewelry show until dark though because one of my girlfriends will be driving, and she buys way more than I do. It'll be 7:30 by the time I can get home. I'll give you a call when I'm on my way and you can come over then."

"Good! Once things are more settled, I'm taking you on a real date again. Until that can happen, I'll be waiting for your call and I'll see you at the townhouse tomorrow night. It can't get here soon enough. Really can't wait to see you! Good night, sweetheart."

Ilana then e-mailed Addison and Amelie to let them know about their Uncle Ib so they'd be prepared to fit some time in for him. After a quick shower, she climbed into her lovely comfortable bed feeling so much better than she had earlier, and earlier had actually been a very short time ago.

I'm so silly! Tarlton really cares, even though he keeps things to himself more than I'd like. Amelie and Addison have the strength and stamina to be doing necessary things, awful as they are. And Ib'll be here soon. It's all good!

Possibly sensing Ilana's need for her to stay close, Blossom licked her hand and settled right beside her bed—something she didn't do every night.

"And, Blossom, maybe the most important thing for me, at this moment, is that you're here."

CHAPTER THIRTY

Amelie's e-mail response to Ilana read: "Uncle Ib is really coming in? It's been years since we've seen him. It was the Christmas of my senior year in high school because I remember he gave me extra money for college. I'm so anxious to see him, and I'll be glad to see you too, but that won't be until this weekend at the grand opening. We're so busy and tired, and I stay so sad seeing the situation, mostly with the birds. We're doing the best we can, and we do get them clean, but we have to face it: they've lost their natural habitat. Anyway, I probably won't get there until grand opening time, so won't see you ahead of time. Addison, Lee, and I'll probably leave here as soon as we can Friday, so we can all go home to get as much rest as possible."

Addison's e-mail response read: "Seems I'll finally be seeing you this weekend for the grand opening. All three of us will be there, but not ahead of time because we'll be trying to rest up as much as possible. I'm so glad to hear about Uncle Ib. It's been too long since we've seen him—maybe a few Christmases before the divorce. This is the first time I've e-mailed anyone other than Marvel and someone interested in buying my place. We're all exhausted when the days end. I hadn't even told you I took a leave from work right after finishing my projects. So much clean-up is needed here, and it's miserably hot work, but there's too much to do to leave it. I do miss work though, and you, and Flex, and everyone. We've made some headway here, but way too much has been lost."

Flex was thrilled when Ilana drove over the next morning to tell him Addison missed him and she did her best to explain how tired he was during his time off. The little guy's special friend hadn't been able to contact him, give him the usual weekly guitar lesson, or hang out with him at all. *Nevertheless,* Flex understood and was impressed and proud that he, Amelie, and Lee—all people he knew—were helping the wildlife. He told her he'd been faithfully practicing his guitar a lot so he'd be able to impress Addison with his playing when he'd finally get to see him.

Ilana found Marvel in her Share-Way office busily formatting grand opening invitations and printing addresses on their envelopes. Ilana knew how she must be missing Addison, but Marvel always managed to stay cheerful as she looked up to say, "Hi Ilana, I figured I could do this beforehand and then only have to fill in the grand opening's date and time when that's confirmed."

"Smart thinking! I thought I might see your dad around here, but Flex says he's running some errands. I'll be seeing him tonight though. Do you have any thoughts on the day and time for the grand-opening? With your input, he and I can maybe decide on a date tonight. Okay?"

"Sounds like a plan! I'd say make it Saturday afternoon, probably from four to ten, in order to accommodate everyone. The younger people will prefer that it be late, but the older ones won't want it late. That's probably the best compromise. Also it'll give Addison, Amelie, and Lee time to get into town. Oh, and you and Dad try to think of anyone I might have forgotten to include."

"Will do! I guess you've talked to the diner guys about eats, but I'll pick up some wine."

"Great! I'll get some beer and ginger ale. That should satisfy everyone without giving them too many choices. Some of the women here have volunteered to make desserts, too. I guess now all we'll need to do is check our stock of paper plates, cups, and utensils and pick up what's needed."

"Okay, let me handle that. Oh, and I'll get napkins. We won't be bothering with tablecloths, right? After all, your dad made sure all this furniture is spill proof. Let's take advantage of it!"

"Right! You be sure to tell him we're grateful for that when you see him tonight."

"Okay, Marvel, seems like we've got it covered. I've wanted to ask you about Addison's e-mail that someone was interested in his place. Have you heard if he sold it? I know they're all at the clean-up site for now, but it has to come to an end sometime, and he'll need to stay somewhere."

"Ilana, there's so much to ask him—if he'll keep his job or fill an eight-hour day here at Share-Way. He's always too exhausted to talk much, so I don't push him on anything. I do know he has a serious buyer who's anxious to hear if and when he can get it. Addison has discovered though, since he's been away, how much he misses his work in architecture. By the way, Ilana, I hear your brother's coming in. I just have to know—is his real name Ib?"

"No," Ilana laughed. "My mother loved to read and discovered the plays of Henrik Ibsen after I was born. When she got pregnant again, she said all along she wanted him named Ibsen if it were a boy. I could only manage to say 'Ib' then, and he liked that better than Ibsen, so it stuck. No one's ever known him by anything but Ib Hayes, and that's how he likes it."

"Now you've got me curious about Henrik Ibsen!"

"I never read any of his plays, so I just know Mom loved the heroines in them. She said he made them real—whether good or bad people—they were genuine. She preferred the most assertive ones because she said those type women were rare in Ibsen's time, the 1800s. Mom was very dramatic. For days she'd quote from something she'd just read, and it was usually something one of those heroines said."

"Hey, now you're making me want to find time to read. I haven't gotten involved in a good book in such a long time. I think I'll do that now that Share-Way's completed. It might even keep me from thinking of Addison so much."

"You know, you're making me realize that I went from decorating here right back into full-time volunteering, without allowing myself time to read. I'd love to wrap my brain around a good book too. But right now, I just need to see your father, Amelie, and Addison again—and now that I know he's coming in, Ib too.

That afternoon Ilana and a girlfriend left Riverside to meet some other friends at a jewelry show, an excellent opportunity for finding great bargains. Although her mind wasn't on much else but seeing Tarlton later, she did manage to get a few Christmas gifts she'd appreciate having when the season came around. She called him on her way home that night as planned and was soon in the townhouse anxiously awaiting the sound of his car in her driveway.

Tarlton walked in behind the prettiest bouquet of red roses Ilana'd ever seen. He set them down on her bar and said, "I don't know if you know what red roses mean, and I only THINK I know, but I mean for them to say 'I love you with everything that's in me.' If you didn't already know it, I'm telling you right now. I want to spend every minute of the rest of my life with you. Can you see yourself doing that? Will you marry me?"

Ilana found the closest chair to collapse into with mouth open and eyes abnormally wide. All she knew to say was, "Give me a sec!"

When she thought about his giving her the framed yellow remnant and beautiful poem months earlier, she realized that was unexpected too. But this? This was a commitment—a proposal—not at all what she would've imagined, especially when he was so busy.

She quickly jumped up to exclaim "Yes, yes! Oh, yes!"

They purposely neglected discussing wedding plans, for that seemed insignificant and would be decided when they got around to it. They wanted to enjoy presently the thought of sharing the rest of their lives together.

"But Tarlton, I should e-mail Amelie and Addison immediately," Ilana said abruptly, consequently breaking the mood.

When Ilana mentioned she wouldn't be in contact with them until they showed up at Share-Way, Tarlton said he'd like to take her on a road trip the next day. He wouldn't divulge the reason, which made her reconsider that she was right that he'd been hiding something—something other than that he was about to propose? How could that be, when he'd been too busy to think of other things?

"Let me take you somewhere tomorrow," he said "to show you something. Actually we'll be picking something up. Uh, oh. I can tell in your eyes, you're thinking it's a ring. No, you'll be picking that out yourself, and we'll do that soon, whenever you like, actually. This is something not that important, but it'll take all day to get to where it is. Are you game?"

"I can't wait!" she answered.

Tarlton was there to pick her up as soon as she returned from church the next morning. They were newly engaged and had a complete day to be together after not having seen each other for, what seemed to both, an eternity, so the day was special, one to be remembered always. They talked some during the ride, smiled over at each other a lot, listened to CDs, and even sang along to familiar lyrics. After driving a long way, they stopped at a road-side diner for a quick lunch. Ilana only then realized they had completely skipped through a state when she saw Alabama on the menu.

"It's not much farther at all," Tarlton assured her, "just a few miles north."

"Apparently you're not giving me any hints. Right?"

"It'd be a waste because you'd guess by the time we'd get there." And he was right to a certain extent, for they soon turned into the driveway of a farm where Ilana spotted a gathering of horses under some pine trees.

"You've bought some horses for Amelie to train and we're here to pick them up. That's it! That's why you only mentioned this after I said I wouldn't see or talk to her until the opening. You thought I'd tell her. Am I right? I'm right, aren't I?"

"Yes, but only partially. Not some horses; I'm only getting two so far, and they're for riding, and don't need taming. We'll only be able to take one today because this guy just has a one-horse trailer, so I'll have to come back again for the other one. Godfrey and Ed are at Share-Way right now building a shelter for them, and we've already got the fenced-in area ready to put one in." He helped her out of the truck and said, "Come on! Let's go meet the beautiful guy we've come to get. He's the most spectacular one around, and I think he looks just like his name: Brazen Sprint!"

****

Ib flew in the following Wednesday afternoon and Ilana met him at Share-Way. They hugged, she cried, and they got caught up, right there in Share-Way's lobby.

"But, Ilana," he suddenly asked, do we know what's the cause of the undertow?"

They laughed almost hysterically as she told him about Brazen Sprint and pointed to the grazing horse through a side window. "He's such a pretty thing! Amelie said she wanted to teach horse-back riding and pleaded with Tarlton from the beginning to have horses here. She even wanted him to buy wild horses so she could break them and train them to be ridden."

"Ha, that's my girl!"

"Oh, you've always been such a fan! She'll be thrilled about it though, that's for sure! Tarlton kept it a secret from me because he was afraid I was so close to her I might let the surprise out. She's such an animal lover! You know that! But she's only ridden horses on vacation. She'd love to teach people to ride horses, but when you think about it, she's barely ridden much herself."

"I don't doubt my little princess will be comfortable riding Brazen Sprint very soon and able to teach horse-back riding in no time. She's my niece, after all!"

"But, Ib, it'll mean her having to make a life-changing decision. She likes her animal research job too, so I don't know if she'll give that up to be here. Tarlton doesn't want to make her feel pressured, so he says he can always find someone for horse-back instruction if she decides to stay with her job. I'm so curious about what she'll decide.

"You know what? There was so much to tell you and I was so happy to see you, I forgot to mention my big news. You're going to have a brother-in-law! Tarlton and I are engaged! I just know you'll be the best of friends. I'll get him to come to the townhouse tomorrow for dinner so you two can meet. Oh, Ib, I'm extremely happy right now. The guys I love most in the world are all going to be around this weekend!"

"I'm so glad you're happy, and congratulations. Tarlton's getting the very best, and I plan to tell him that. From what you've told me about him, I think he might meet my specifications."

"If I haven't told you how great it is to have you here, IT IS!" she squealed as she pinched him and tugged at his arm in persuasion. "Come on, you big lug! Let me show you around Share-Way—first the outside—SINCE YOU PAID FOR IT—and before it gets dark. Get ready! You'll love what you'll see on this tour, outside and in. It's all fabulous, and Tarlton has thought of everything."

****

Tarlton and Ib hit it off well at their get-acquainted dinner, as Ilana expected they would. They talked about the marines, of course, and Ib's travels, Share-Way and New Orleans, with each fascinated by the other's experiences.

As they sat down to dinner, Tarlton asked, "So, Ib, is there a special woman in your life right now?"

"Now, what is it with you engaged guys? You want the rest of us tied down as soon as you are. There's no special woman in my life. There are a FEW women actually, but none I'd want to spend more than an evening with. I guess you got the last special one. Anyway, man, you know how it is, I've gotten older and kind of set in my ways."

With a straight, sincere face, Tarlton looked squarely at him and said seriously, "Ib, you're younger than I am. I might've been set in my ways too, but I've finally found the love of my life and I know now that for the right woman, we adjust."

"I'll remember that, I promise. I've just been busy with work and travel and no one's ever set a fire under me that way, you know? Anyway, I've been just about everywhere, so if there's a right woman for me, I should've come across her by now. She's running out of places to show up!"

The phone rang. Ilana excused herself, picked it up, and heard screaming, happy screaming. "Mom," Addison said, "you're not the only one in the family engaged. Marvel's agreed to marry me. We figured Tarlton would be with you and wanted you both to know. As far as plans go, I decided to stay in architecture, and Marvel will continue handling bills and paper work at Share-Way. I'm going to look for work close to Riverside and we'll also start looking for a house there."

Ilana screamed, then congratulated them both with her best wishes and blessings. She then put Tarlton on the phone, who did the same, except without the screaming.

CHAPTER THIRTY-ONE

In order to make the best of the limited amount of time he'd have to be in town, Ib took advantage of what he considered his second priority, seeing New Orleans and getting to know its people. Tarlton and Ilana took him around somewhat, but one night and a few afternoons, he and his rental car had to wing it alone. He began to sense a sincere love for the people and their welcoming spirit gradually developing inside him. *Nevertheless,* he kept it to himself as long as he could.

Since Ib had first arrived, he and Ilana had quickly gotten into the habit of sharing breakfasts that she insisted on fixing him every day. It soon became the only time they were sure they'd see each so they resorted to leaving each other nightly refrigerator messages so they could have that time together with no conflicts.

"You know, Sis," Ib mentioned sleepily one morning early as he poured his coffee, "what makes this short visit incomplete is that I'm not getting to see Addison and Amelie. What fun it'd be to have my niece and nephew show me the best places to go in New Orleans! Even though they both live away, I'm sure they stay familiar enough with it to know the more fun spots."

"I guess you're probably right about that, but you'll only get to see them Saturday at Share-Way's grand opening. I'm not sure when their work leaves are up, but there can't be much time left before they have to get back to their regular jobs. You'll just have to come in again, and soon!"

"They've become successful people since I've seen them, Sis. You did good!"

"Thanks! I am proud of them, more than I can say!"

"And I get the feeling from you and Tarlton that everyone gets along well—like family. Amelie and Addison can never have enough father figures around, you know?"

"That seems odd coming from you. They don't see their dad a lot, but he's in their lives. You know that. What do you mean by father figures?"

"Like uncles, for instance. You'll catch on soon to the undertow, so I guess I should explain."

"Ib Hayes," she laughed as she stopped stirring her coffee, "you've been here just long enough that any undertow you've caused wouldn't surprise me one bit. What've you done?"

"Nothing, it's not anything I've done, but what I'm thinking about doing. Look, this is the way I've got it figured. You and Tarlton will get married soon and move into his place in the Marigny. Then, the only person in charge at Share-Way, on a constant basis, will be Marvel. What if there's a problem? Who'd be around to handle it?"

"But, Ib, you know Tarlton will be at Share-Way more than at his place, at least in the beginning. And Marvel will have him on speed dial. Anyway, there are many healthy, able, and ready young men there—the foster home kids and the one from Lark's rental house. We don't really anticipate problems. Why? What're you thinking could happen?"

"You never know—an obnoxious visiting relative, someone's boss claiming he's owed more work time, an irate ex-husband. Now, I hope things will go smoothly, of course, but...well, Sis, Share-Way needs someone around who could be tough and intimidating—you know, someone no one would want to mess with."

"But...what do you mean? Like who?" She studied the look on his face and knew right away to ask, "You're thinking it's you? You're thinking of staying? You mean you would...."

"Sis, do you think I could be of any help at Share-Way?"

She grabbed his hand across the table and quickly answered, "Oh, Tarlton could find more than enough for you to handle. Are you truly serious?"

"Well, I've just been thinking maybe I don't need to stay in the marines any longer. When Flex had me telling him what it was like to be in the military the other day, it got me to thinking that I've been in since right out of high school. I guess I've been waiting for a reason to finally retire. It's been a great run! But you and Amelie and Addison, and soon Tarlton and Marvel, are my family. And families are what're important. I've come to appreciate everything about New Orleans, too, and I like living here close to it. I'd be looking for someplace temporary anyway, and it could just as well be at Share-Way, if I'm welcome. Don't you see? I want to be around y'all. Gees! Already I'm talking like everyone around here!"

"Ib, your being around would make my life absolutely complete! I can't see how it could be better," and she squeezed his hand tighter, as if to press her love into it. "Let's call Tarlton!"

"Maybe that should wait for now. Let it spin around in your head a while and see if you can come up with any drawback to this idea. But, I know you're going to tell Tarlton immediately, the instant you see or talk to him, right?"

"Yes, I probably will, but only because I'm so excited. Oh, but wait! I know how you are. You're liable to change your mind about this. You've been known to have ideas that fizzled quickly when you lost interest. So, for my own good, I'm going to purposely avoid thinking about this and focus entirely on the grand opening. As of now, it's off my mind completely By the way, I'll be going over to Share-Way a little later to finalize some things with Marvel. Do you want to come?"

"I'm in. Yes. Since I've only been there once, my going over there now, when it's early and before much activity starts, will give me a better feel for the place—I mean from the perspective of it being a possible living arrangement. Godfrey, Ed, and I are leaving around 10:00 for the World War II Museum, and Ed's driving, so I can ride over there with you and get Ed to bring me back here after. Just give me a minute."

When they were both ready for the day, they met again at Ilana's front door. Ib kissed her cheek and said, "Now, remember, you're only concentrating on the grand opening."

"While I was getting ready, it occurred to me how thrilled Flex will be to hear you'd be at Share-Way. He thinks you're so cool! But I'm not thinking about it—no, only about the opening!"

"Keep that thought! But I have to say, Sis, that kid's been through so much and yet he's so well-adjusted now. Accolades to Godfrey and all of you who had a hand in accomplishing that! Now, today you only think of the opening, remember! Okay, Let's roll!"

****

That night Tarlton called and asked Ib to drive to Alabama with him the following day to pick up the other horse; consequently, the second trip wasn't quite as romantic as the first. After leaving early, they drove through spotty showers most of the way, but it was a time for further bonding.

"I should thank you again, Ib, for your generous contribution for Share-Way's exterior, and especially the pool. Actually my not having those expenses is why I'm able to buy these horses and all that's needed to have them—that and the fact that we didn't have to buy as much furniture for the lobby since we used what was salvaged and redone of my Mom's furniture. And, now that I think of it, not having to pay for storing all that furniture anymore is a bonus."

"Man, what would I have done with that money? I'm just glad I had it."

"I have to confess, Ib. I'm a little worried about this horse. He's not as calm as what you've seen of Brazen Sprint. He might not even be willing to get in the trailer. I figured it might upset Ilana to see him resisting, so I'm glad you were able to come with me instead."

"Oh, we can handle getting him in the trailer. It might take some extra effort, but we can do it. By the way, I'm pretty good with horses!"

"Really? That's great, because I haven't had many opportunities to be around them."

"And also, I don't mind being your second choice for this trip—as long as you don't make me ride in the trailer. By the way, Tarlton, I can swim too!"

"What?" Tarlton asked, awkwardly puzzled, as he turned to look in Ib's direction.

"I said I can swim! Tarlton. I can dive, handle water rescue, ride horses, work with kids, and I'm military, so I tend to be able to keep things running smoothly."

"So?"

"Man, are you going to make me spell it out? I think I could do some good at Share-Way."

"You mean you'd...." Tarlton pulled the car to the side of the road. "Give me that again."

"I'm thinking I could help out. I'd really like to be closer to Ilana and the kids, and I'd have to find a place to stay anyway. Bottom line, Tarlton—this is the first time I've ever had the urge to retire from the marines."

"Well, that's fabulous, although I admit I have to wrap my brain around that idea. I didn't have a clue. I wonder why Ilana hasn't mentioned it, or have you told her?"

"Oh, yes, I did, but just yesterday. She knows how I can flip around on things though."

"How do you mean?"

"She's known me to lose interest in things and waver before making a definite decision."

"Uh, oh, but assuming you're better at that now, we certainly could use you."

"Great! And yes, I'm certainly better. I just had to mature. Sisters tend to recall only the dumbest things their brothers did when they were young and relish embarrassing them with it at every possible opportunity."

Tarlton smiled, started the car, and merged into traffic again as he said, "You know, Marvel says Addison is willing to give music lessons and help out with swimming, and he'll do any electronic repairs, but I was really counting on having him full time. Yes, it'll be good having you at Share-Way, even if you end up with an apartment in New Orleans, which will probably happen eventually. I never would've thought you'd be interested in doing this—not ever. You're so...so...military!"

"That I am, but not TOO military. And there are so many things I want to do around the area—go to some Saints and Hornets games, ride on the ferry, do some bayou fishing, ride a horse on the levee, and even visit some churches. It's time I got in touch with my spiritual side. I've been reading the Bible lately, too. Now, you be sure to tell Ilana I said that! She'll be pretty impressed!"

"Wow! That might be the most shocking thing to come out of this surprise of yours!"

They laughed and rode quietly for a while, until Tarlton said, "You know what? The more I think about it, you might be exactly what Share-Way needs to get it headed in the right direction. After all, I've heard the marines can do it all!"

"Pretty much! We're trained that way all right. I know I'm getting older, but I feel like I could handle anything."

"But, Ib, your retiring and relocating—that's such an important step. So you don't make too hasty a decision, it's probably best that you get back to your usual routine at home where you can think more objectively. I won't count on you until I hear something definite from you from there."

"Good deal! As far as I'm concerned though, I could give you that definite right now because I can easily picture myself at Share-Way. I already think the world of Godfrey and Ed, and Flex is a great kid. I want to spend a lot of time on the levee with him looking out at the river, and have him tell me all about his fascination with it."

"What he says he loves too is that, from the upstairs windows at my house, he can see freighters passing on the river. If Ilana and I notice him not around, we're sure to find him up there, just sitting and watching. But I understand his fascination with the levee and want to be out there more myself. Of course there are barges parked along the levee that block the river view somewhat, but I know the necessity for having them there. More commerce passes up and down the Mississippi than people realize. New Orleans is an extremely important port. I'll have to tell you about it sometime."

"New Orleans is important for more than just the port, man. The people I've met in New Orleans and those Ilana's introduced me to here on this side of the river are so warm and friendly. I must say though, I might have to stay clear of the older women at Share-Way. I notice a couple of them seem a little too warm and friendly."

CHAPTER THIRTY-TWO

Ilana was alarmed by Amelie's frantic voice on the phone early Saturday morning. Frightening thoughts immediately came to mind but she forced herself to stay calm and listen as Amelie said, "Mom, I'm about to get in the car to head over to Riverside and I've got to see you ahead of time before I see everyone else at the grand opening. I'm so mixed up and torn and….."

"Oh, Sweetie, what's happening?"

"It's my whole situation, Mom—leaving all that still needs doing over here, my job, Lee, my feelings for him, his wanting me to work with the environment full time. I don't know if I should just chuck it all to enjoy horses at Share-Way. Oh, I've never felt so mixed up."

"It's so good to hear your voice. It's been too long, but I surely don't want you to be this upset. Come as soon as you get to town if you want. It must have been traumatic facing suffering animals and having to clean and get them healthy in enough time to save them. It's bound to get to you, especially if there's been some pressure—of any kind—from Lee."

"I guess. But there's been no one to talk to about anything. Of course, there's been no time to talk about anything either, only what needs to be done, and the oil, and the birds, and the turtles, and…Oh, I feel so guilty for leaving, but I just have to get away from here."

"Then I'll be here waiting for you and I'll have something for you to eat. Uncle Ib will be looking forward to seeing you, of course, but I'll send him off somewhere so you and I can have some time by ourselves. Now, Amelie, have you gotten enough sleep?"

"Yes, I got plenty of rest last night. Actually as soon as we finished yesterday, I went and filled my gas tank, came here, showered, gobbled something down, and hit the bed. Luckily, when I was home last week-end, I thought ahead to bring something to wear at Share-Way, so I'll be coming right to Riverside without going to my place. I planned to leave early so I'd get there with time to spare. Oh, Mom, it's all so sad over here."

"I can imagine, Sweetie, and we're all very proud of you for doing it. Now, you need some quiet time alone to clear your thoughts, and interstate driving will give you that, to a certain extent. When you get everything loaded up and ready to leave, put a soft music tape in and don't worry about deciding anything. Just let your mind be free—but don't get distracted from your driving. Please keep your eyes on the road. By the time you get here, I have a feeling your mind will be much more open to making decisions."

"Oh, I hope so. Now my mind's crammed with only the damage an oil rig explosion can do."

"Do Lee and Addison know when you were planning to leave? Because not having your phone buzzing would help to keep you undisturbed."

"Yes, I said my goodbyes to everyone yesterday when I left there, and I think I was the first to leave. They both knew I was heading out early and wouldn't be seeing them again until we'd meet at Share-Way. I'm about ready to get on the road. I've just got to make a last run to the bathroom, grab a low-cal soda, and I'm out of here—and good riddance."

"Now you be careful and I'll be looking for you late morning sometime, but don't speed. Bye, and I love you."

Amelie hung up, double-checked her room for anything she'd overlooked, and closed the door quietly to avoid disturbing her roommates anymore than she already had. As she put some things on the floor in the car's back seat, settled into the driver's seat, and found an appropriate tape, she began to realize how long it had been since she'd thought of Share-Way—or anything else except fighting oil—for that matter. At this point, any thought meandering its way into her mind was a thought to be cherished. A streetlight provided only a slight amount of illumination, so she started the engine knowing that, at this early hour, she could cover a lot of interstate before any signs of daylight would appear.

Amelie was content—and extremely proud—of what she and her co-workers had accomplished toward helping animals and mankind during her past five years in research. Now it seemed such a meager contribution in comparison to the dedication, energy, and time the people she'd just worked with were willing to devote to it. She felt such strong admiration for them—especially Lee—who might be the most dedicated of them all.

Before long, a clear yet overcast day began to develop, the kind Amelie considered the absolute best for driving because of the absence of glare. Her contact lenses always made glare extremely bothersome for her. To now be driving in comfort without it seemed like a sign to her that things might already be going her way.

By the time the sun was up, Amelie was already half-way to Riverside and feeling as if her senses were experiencing a sort of euphoria in the way they absorbed everything around her. The colors of road signs and trees she passed seemed more pronounced, and each individual musical CD note swelled clearer than she'd ever noticed. She released the laughter bubbling inside her, joyful and freeing laughter, when she realized even her sense of smell was affected. Though her car was her second home in a way, she'd never before had her lemon-scented car deodorizer make her crave a lemon snowball.

She soon felt the urge to replace her quiet CDs with Bob Dylan's, the one that contained "Blowin' in the Wind." It brought back memories of her teen-age discussions with her mother about the years she'd have to exist before she was allowed to be free. All Amelie knew for sure was that she wanted, no—needed, a trauma-free life again. But, did she want that life to include Lee? How could she attempt to answer that until they could be together under normal, 'non-devastation-type' circumstances? They'd never really been on a date. It seemed she could only recall their time together at environmental conferences or studying area coastal maps—and none ever included a glass of wine.

****

Flex and a few baseball buddies were beginning a neighborhood game on Share-Way's lawn while Godfrey, Ed, and some other residents watched from under the oak tree. They were enjoying their second cups of coffee while Chicory waited close by to lick their cups clean. All looked up as Lee's truck swerved into Share-Way's drive-way as he called from his truck window, "Where's Amelie? I don't see her car."

"Well, good mornin', Lee," Godfrey answered as he walked toward the truck. "Haven't seen her, son. As far as we know, she's been with you and the turtles. What do ya think of the place?"

"Oh, it looks fabulous, Godfrey, really, but I've got to talk to Amelie. She said she'd leave extra early, so I didn't see her this morning. I was sure she'd be here helping to get things ready. I'd better call her."

"My guess is she's at her mom's," Ed piped in as he also approached. "They haven't seen each other since this whole oil mess started. Why don't you meet us in the kitchen for some coffee and we'll give you a special tour before everyone shows up?"

Lee parked as Godfrey and Ed walked toward his truck, and when they were close enough, they heard him say, "Where are you? Are you okay? I'm at Share-Way looking for you."

"I'll see you later, Lee. I'm at Mom's and I'm fine."

"But, will you be coming back to work with us? It sounded like you wouldn't."

"No, I won't! I'm more sorry than I can say, but I just can't do that any longer. I admire your wanting to, and I know everything about you says you have to, but I just can't. I don't know if I'll go back to my job, or help out at Share-Way, now that I know they'll have horses. I don't know what I'll do, but I can't handle the oil clean-up any longer. I'm sorry."

"Amelie, let's talk about this. What's going on? I thought we shared something...I can't believe...We'll still see each other, right?"

"Lee, I'll see you at Share-Way. I'll be my friendly self. How about you call and ask me out sometime? I guess I'd like to spend some fun time with you and see where it goes."

"But I thought you felt as strongly as I do about us. What's happened?"

"Lee, we need to share normal situations, like dinner and a movie, or dancing, or going to a concert or a ballgame, or even just having drinks. I'd really love doing any of those things with you. Meantime, I'll see you later. I've gotta go. Bye now."

"Wh...She hung up! Now what?" he said as he looked from Ed to Godfrey.

"You come along with us, that's what," Ed said while taking his arm and leading him toward the building. "You'll see her later. Women are hard to figure. Anyway, you know, Lee, I'm not much of a reader, but I like how Robert Frost thought. Someone told me he once summed up his thoughts on life in three words: 'It goes on!'"

"Right!" Godfrey added. "Now, to help you get your mind off womenfolk, let's go see your dad. Mr. B's been drivin' us crazy he's so anxious to see you!"

****

Grand opening time soon arrived and many wide-eyed, awe-struck people wandered around Share-Way. It was no longer a dream! It was a real building, an absolute finite structure that would actually house people and keep them content and fulfilled for a long time. This particular afternoon, its entire atmosphere seemed to be permeated in bliss. Jubilation exuded from the hearts of the residents and seemed to bounce off the freshly-painted walls. Smiles were everywhere—well, except maybe on Lee Bienvenu's face.

When someone from the local paper approached Tarlton for a personal comment, he declared loudly; "I feel triumphant because it's been a long time coming. It's been a collaborative effort that utilized many talents, and I don't think I could be happier."

While the younger residents passed around refreshments, the older residents proudly showed off every inch of the building to their friends and families. The following comments could be heard if one mingled among the groups and listened closely:

"I can't wait to get in the pool. Dude, we'll even get lessons!"

"We can get our hair cut without even having to leave here."

"Staying here while working will give me a chance to save for college."

"Well, my favorite is having people to play bridge and canasta with..."

"I'm going to learn to play the guitar, Dude. I can't wait."

"How about that mural on the wall! You're looking at who did it!"

"I tell you what...nothing beats sitting under the old oak tree..."

"I love being able to mess around with that piano..."

"Tending to young-uns again has made my life complete..."

"The white table to do jigsaw puzzles on is the best. I can see the pieces..."

"Addison's gonna help me fix up my van until I can get something better."

"I'm dying to play pickle ball; don't know what it is, but I want to play..."

"You know, Godfrey and Ed whip up some mighty good meals..."

"We display pictures from our grandkids under the glass of that table..."

"I'm planning to learn calligraphy and make money on doing invitations."

"Hey, y'all, somebody's gonna teach me to hip hop in my wheelchair!"

Portions of pecan pie and rum-covered bread pudding were set out on tables, which were then protected from canine residents eyeing the culinary masterpieces. At future gatherings, perhaps animals would remain in rooms or be put in the fenced-in outer yard—one of many lessons to be learned while moving forward. However, sincere camaraderie permeated the toasts, high fives, handshakes, and hugs in this night's spirited celebration of unity and optimism—the first of many.

As Share-Way's construction advanced, minds and hearts were gradually purged of past disappointments. It's completion now guaranteed those minds and hearts an opportunity to dream. Here was verification that with wise planning and diligence, hopes can *nevertheless* become *everthemore.*